THE RIGHT CHOICE

NEW YORK TIMES BESTSELLING AUTHOR
Carly Phillips

Copyright © Karen Drogin 2014
Print Edition
CP Publishing 2014
Cover Design: The Killion Group Inc.

Will she make the right choice...

Advice columnist Carly Wexler has mapped out her entire life, and she's convinced by marrying her best friend, she'll be able to map out her path to happiness as well. No sexual sparks? No problem. Or so she thinks...until her fiance's brother arrives for the wedding. Mike Novak ignites a desire inside Carly unlike anything she's ever experienced, shaking up everything she's ever believed in. When Mike becomes determined to stop her mismatched wedding to his brother, will Carly be able to accept that her unexpected love for Mike might be the right choice for her after all?

* * *

Dear Readers,

Welcome to "Carly Classics", books I wrote earlier in my career that have been modernized for your reading enjoyment. These stories hold a very special place in my heart and I'm thrilled to be able to share them with you now.

All the best,
Carly

ONE

C arly Wexler stood back and admired the window display. Rays of sunlight streamed through the plate glass, illuminating an assortment of gold and diamond wedding bands. The enduring symbols of love and commitment caused her stomach to bunch into a tight knot. She closed her eyes, firmly convinced that a fresh glance at the sparkling rings would calm her nerves. After all, nothing could go wrong when a wedding had been planned as meticulously as hers.

She opened her eyes for another look. To her left, complementary wedding bands shimmered against a black velvet backdrop. His and hers. Carly and Peter. They were, as her fiancé reminded her, well-suited, sharing mutual friends and interests. A matched set, she thought, her gaze drifting over the glittering selections.

Every piece in the window had a partner... an apt description of her relationship with her fiancé. They didn't share a grand passion, but that was what made theirs a perfect union. In an ideal world, love and passion could coexist, making a couple a perfect fit, instead of merely offering them a perfect coexistence. But Carly no longer believed in fairy tales. Thanks to her father's destructive actions, she had seen the damage running on pure emotion could cause. Better to accept mutual respect and caring than to risk pain and disillusionment. She brushed at her newly cut bangs, paying little attention when they fell forward again.

A plain platinum and 18-karat gold set caught her eye. Though the crisscrossed bands were flanked on either side by more jeweled rings, Carly couldn't take her eyes off the simpler pair. "Perfect," she murmured. Too bad her fiancé would prefer a ring with more precious stones, one designed to impress.

"Like those." She tapped her finger against the window.

She understood Peter's need to make a statement, just as he understood her need for the perfect wedding with all the trimmings. Give and take, she reminded herself. Her finger traced a pattern on the cool glass.

"What woman wouldn't like all those glittering diamonds?" From directly behind her, a sexy yet unfamiliar voice vibrated in her ear.

The question intrigued her. "One with substance perhaps?" She answered without turning. Both her heart and her gaze had refocused on her ring of choice.

"And wit," the man added with obvious admiration.

She clasped her hands behind her back. "Good taste," she responded, enjoying the innocent game.

The answering chuckle, deep and resonant, captured her interest, diverting her from choosing the circular band that would forever bind her to her future husband.

"It takes brains to see beyond the dazzle of diamonds," the stranger said, approval marking his masculine drawl.

"I suppose." Curiosity aroused, she turned toward the voice, her long skirt floating around her bare legs as she moved.

The sensual voice tantalized but hadn't deceived. A ruggedly handsome man smiled at her. Her gaze locked with his. Hazel eyes flecked with gold shimmered beneath the afternoon sun and laugh lines bracketed a sensuous mouth.

Those mesmerizing eyes studied her intently. "Real beauty speaks for itself."

Her cheeks heated at the unexpected compliment. "Thank you," she murmured.

"Just stating the obvious."

Embarrassed, Carly acknowledged his words with a nod. She felt a connection with this stranger, one that defied logic. With long sandy hair streaked by the sun and the sexy way he rocked on the heels of worn hiking boots, he oozed wildness and danger, raw masculinity and cocky confidence. She brushed at her bangs with trembling hands. She preferred tame and safe. This man was anything but.

"So, what attracts you?" he asked. His gaze lingered on her an instant too long before darting to the jewel-filled window.

You do. The unbidden thought rocketed through her brain. "Those," she said in a hoarse croak. She pointed to the simple bands with a none too steady hand.

"Nice," he murmured in agreement. "So have we discovered what kind of woman prefers plain gold to diamonds?" His rich laugh hung in the air.

The sound warmed her, even as an unexpected chill dashed over her skin. She glanced up at the blue sky. A single puff of cloud covered the sun. Carly knew with complete certainty that this man, and not a passing feat of nature, caused her tremors and a distinct feeling of unease.

"Someone with more sense than to stand on a street corner in Manhattan and talk to a perfect stranger," she murmured. "Excuse me." She pivoted on her heel, intending to head inside the store, where safety in numbers awaited her.

"Carly, wait."

She froze in midflight, turning back toward that compelling voice. "Who are you?" she asked warily.

"Mike Novack, Peter's brother." He held a bronzed hand toward her.

She silently cursed her fiancé's lack of sentiment. The only picture she'd seen of Mike had been as a young boy. Certainly she'd have recalled seeing a current photo of the good-looking man standing before her.

"Brother." Even as she reached out her hand, dismay and self-loathing rippled through her. Flirting with a stranger while shopping for wedding bands had been bad enough, but flirting with Peter's errant brother showed a decided lack of judgment.

The type of judgment she'd expect from her father, not from herself.

"Last time I checked," Mike said.

His strong hand grasped hers and she lost any sense of equilibrium she might have felt. His calloused fingers wrapped around her skin, enclosing her hand in warmth.

Heat traveled from her fingers, up her arm and into her breasts before settling in the pit of her stomach. Through sheer force of will, she tried to ignore the new and unnerving sensations.

She wrenched her hand free from Mike's grasp and

focused all her attention on the plate-glass window. Without the sun's rays, the rings had lost much of their sparkle and allure. She wrapped her arms across her chest in a futile attempt to warm herself inside and out.

"Carly?"

She grit her teeth against the sound of concern in his deep voice. "Obviously you've seen my picture."

Mike smiled. "The one on Peter's desk."

"I wish I could say the same of you."

"I'm the photographer in the family, not Pete."

"So I've heard. Are you also the family flirt?"

His eyes narrowed in confusion. "I know I've been out of the country for a while, but when did casual conversation become slang for come-on?"

She blew her bangs out of her eyes with a hard puff of air. "Okay, I overreacted." To a man who made her heart race and her palms sweat. As far as she was concerned, she'd definitely underreacted.

She really wanted to run and hide from Mike and from herself. "Truce?" she asked, holding out her hand. To prove she could handle physical contact, not because she craved the sensations his warm touch aroused.

"Truce." Mike grasped and released her hand in a quick movement. She wondered if it was because he realized that his mere presence had obviously left her shaken.

"Where is Peter?" Carly asked.

"Work. He was on his way out the door when a last minute crisis hit. He sent me along with his apologies."

"Lawyers." The nonchalant shrug of her shoulders was at distinct odds with the disappointed look in her eyes. "At least this time he remembered to send someone to tell me, even though he could've called or texted me." She smiled. "Thank you."

* * *

"My pleasure," he said. The woman standing before Mike was a definite surprise.

When he had asked about Carly, his brother had answered with a distracted, "We're two of a kind, a match made in professional heaven." To Mike, the answer had been the equivalent of "She's got a good personality." Never a rave review for a woman. Mike had then sought answers in the framed picture on Peter's desk. The black-and-white photo hadn't done justice to this woman.

Perhaps she wasn't a knockout, but she definitely possessed a certain something that made a man look twice. An elusive quality he'd like to capture on film. Light brown hair with golden highlights framed her face and caressed her shoulders in soft waves. Wispy bangs fell just below her eyebrows—when she wasn't swiping at them with one hand. Mike suppressed the urge to brush them aside, just to see if her hair felt as soft as it looked. Her lips were a bit too full but glistened enticingly beneath a sheen of pink gloss.

His brother was one lucky SOB. Not that Mike would ever trade his freedom for the confines of marriage, but he intended to make sure Peter appreciated his good fortune.

"Mike?"

A tap on his shoulder took him by surprise and he flinched.

"Are you okay?" she asked.

"Fine." He rolled his shoulder in a circle, stretching the tight muscles. He wondered if the recent injury would ever heal, or if the ache, along with the scars, were meant as a permanent reminder of what he'd left behind and all he still had to go back to.

"I asked how much time we've got," as she lifted one eyebrow in question.

"About…" He glanced at his watch. "Another five, ten minutes, depending on whether or not Pete gets sidetracked. If he's not here by a quarter after, he said to consider him a no-show and he'll call to reschedule." He grinned. "His words, not mine."

"Not a problem. It's nothing unusual anyway."

Awfully accepting for a woman waiting to pick

wedding bands with her beloved fiancé, Mike thought. "I see Pete still treats his personal life like a business meeting."

"Don't judge him." Her eyes narrowed, flashing angry sparks.

Her defense of her fiancé was admirable, if undeserved, Mike thought.

"Lawyers' hours are unpredictable. I understand."

"So do I." But if his driven, workaholic brother often ignored Carly in favor of legal briefs and pestering clients, he needed a libido transplant.

"He wanted to be here," she said.

"I never said otherwise. I just said he hasn't changed."

A muscle twitched in her cheek for a second before she gave in and smiled. "I guess you do know your brother well."

"You sound surprised."

"It's just that he's always concerned about you, but you're…" She trailed off. A slight flush stained her cheeks, painting them a rosy pink.

"Rarely in touch," he finished for her. "Comes with the territory. The places I travel lack the luxury of pre-paid cell phones."

"But the two of you are close."

"We're brothers." For Mike, that said it all. But for each other, Mike and Peter had no one else in the world who cared. Except Carly. Peter now had his fiancé and Mike had to stop staring at her as if he'd discovered uncharted territory. Better to concentrate on the upcoming wedding and lifelong commitment between Carly and his brother.

"How long will you be in town?" she asked.

"At least the month until the wedding and probably awhile afterward. Then I hit the road again." He had no other choice. He'd left mid-assignment because he'd allowed personal demons to haunt him. He knew damn well he had to face them down if he wanted to look himself in the mirror every morning. Mike Novack never left a job undone, and the man he knew himself to be wouldn't let the past haunt him.

Once he returned to the rambling life he'd always loved, everything would get back to normal…or so he hoped, as he glanced at the woman about to marry his brother.

"Ready to check out the rings inside?" Mike asked.

"Sure." But her gaze strayed to the jewel-filled window once again.

"Is there one you really like?" he asked.

"Those." She leaned forward and tapped lightly, indicating a set of simple two-toned rings.

A woman with substance. His mind ran through their earlier banter and he realized she'd meant every word. "They're beautiful," he said.

She turned to look at him. "But not Peter's taste." A frown touched her lips and a corresponding sadness flashed in her gentle brown eyes.

"You're right. They wouldn't stop traffic. Pete would prefer something a little more… noticeable."

She sighed.

"You obviously know him well, too," Mike said.

She smiled. "We understand each other."

Did they? Mike had spent but a few minutes with each and he'd already begun to wonder. Watching Carly stare longingly at the rings in the window, he grew concerned.

"It's getting late," she murmured. "I hope he realizes these things can't be rushed and we have to have them ordered, sized and engraved. Then there are the tuxedos, the final flower arrangements, the…"

"Relax. No list is set in stone. It'll all get done in time."

"Only if we follow my schedule."

Mike placed a comforting hand on her bare shoulder, realizing his mistake too late. Her skin felt like fine silk beneath his roughened fingers. He breathed in deeply. She looked like sunshine and smelled like vanilla. A potent combination, he discovered.

"What if we get a cup of coffee and go over this schedule of yours? I'm sure you'd relax once you see everything will fall into place."

Her frantic gaze darted from his hand, which remained on her shoulder, to the rings in the storefront window. "Coffee's not such a good idea."

He ought to let her go. After his overwhelming reaction to her, distance seemed the safest route. "We've got the time," he muttered instead.

"Pick up any magazine or newspaper. Caffeine's not good for you." She stepped toward the street. Before he realized her intent, a yellow taxi screeched to a halt.

"Thanks for meeting me. I'm sure with all the wedding things going on I'll be seeing a lot more of you." Her rambling clearly stated that she hoped that wouldn't be the case. Those huge brown eyes told another story.

"Count on it," he said with a smile.

No sooner had she darted into the waiting cab than the taxi pulled away from the curb.

"Ah, the joys of living in New York City." He watched as the brake lights disappeared into the maze of traffic, taking Carly farther away.

* * *

Carly stepped into the familiar lobby of Peter's building. The smell of fresh paint permeated the air. Clean white walls surrounded chrome and mirrors. She wasn't surprised. Thanks to the cost of the apartment and the condominium fees, the tenants in this Upper East Side luxury building demanded quality service and maintenance. Peter was no exception.

"Evening, Miss Wexler."

"Hi, George." Carly smiled at the gray-haired doorman she'd known as long as she'd known Peter. "Is he in?" she asked.

"Flew past me not ten minutes ago."

"Good. Do me a favor, don't announce me." She leaned closer to the small desk. "I want to surprise him."

The older man grinned. "Not a problem. You be good," he said with a laugh.

"I always am. Thanks, George. And you have a nice night." With a wave, she headed for the bank of elevators at the far end of the hall.

In the normal course of events, Carly went out of her way not to surprise Peter, but his schedule had been decidedly uncooperative lately.

The elevator doors glided open and Carly stepped inside. Since her engagement, she'd given the wedding planning "experts" free rein. In her role as columnist and counselor, others relied on Carly for advice, but in her personal life she had no problem deferring to those more experienced than her... especially now. She'd made a commitment, and vows were something she intended to repeat only once in this lifetime.

She stepped out of the elevator and walked down the familiar hallway, pausing outside Peter's apartment. A rush of panic hit her and she wished she'd called first.

Too late. She rapped lightly on the door.

"Coming." The muffled voice was followed by heavy footsteps and the rattle of a chain lock.

"You guys are late and I'm starving." The door swung open wide. "You're not the pizza man."

Carly swallowed hard. "And you're not Peter." She hadn't expected to see Mike again without being forewarned. Nor had she expected the adrenaline rush to be quite so potent the second time.

"Thankfully, no. I'm much more laid-back and a heck of a lot better-looking."

"All ego," she said, suppressing a grin.

"Not enough substance?" Mike asked.

Too much, she thought, as they fell into the easy banter of earlier that afternoon.

He gestured her inside. Carly stepped past him. The warm aroma of spiced aftershave assaulted her senses, heightening her awareness of the man standing in the entryway. Behind her, the apartment door closed with a heavy thud. She turned to find Mike leaning, one shoulder propped against the wall. One bare muscular shoulder. A shudder rippled through her, catching her unaware.

"Did you decide to take me up on that cup of coffee?" he asked with a knowing grin.

She fingered her bangs. "I'd forgotten all about it"

She hadn't forgotten him, though. In fact, she'd spent the rest of the day attempting to push all thoughts of Mike Novack out of her mind.

He walked toward her, forcing her to acknowledge that she'd been unsuccessful in her attempt. "I'm disappointed," he said. "But you can make up for your lack of concern by sharing my pizza." His gaze never wavered.

Golden eyes captured her, making her feel cornered. Light-headed. Excited. She anticipated the rush that came with their verbal sparring.

He tapped the tip of her nose with one finger. "I hate eating alone."

"I'll bet you rarely do," she muttered.

A cough jolted Carly into sudden awareness of her surroundings. She jerked away from Mike, feeling a mixture of guilt and lingering desire.

"This is a surprise," Peter said, watching them both from a few feet away.

"Not an unwelcome one, I'm sure." Mike walked past her and seated himself on the sleek leather couch in the living room. He propped his feet on a glass cocktail table and crossed his arms over his chest.

"Of course not," Peter said. He smiled and extended a hand toward Carly. She went to him, trying to ignore the feel of Mike's burning gaze. She brushed a kiss on Peter's damp cheek. Freshly showered, he smelled of familiar soap and shampoo. He drew her against him, resting his arm around her waist. "Carly's always welcome. This visit just wasn't planned."

Carly grinned and elbowed him in the ribs. "Since planning hasn't worked, I decided to ambush you instead. Look." She patted the bag that hung from her shoulder, bulging with lists and articles from the most recent wedding magazines.

Peter groaned. Looking thoroughly put out and grumbling about neurotic women, he allowed Carly to lead him to the couch and push him onto the cushion beside Mike. She knew better than to be insulted. Long before they'd gotten engaged, she and Peter had been friends. He understood her even when she drove him to sheer exasperation with her never-ending lists and articles. Besides, they shared the same goal— marriage and the perks that came with it.

For Carly, those perks included stability and security. For Peter, she sensed their engagement had more to do with her solid support as he climbed the ladder toward partnership. When all was said and done, they wanted the same things, even if their dreams were a little different.

"Ready to get started?" She knelt down beside her

fiancé.

"Go for it," Mike said.

She chuckled aloud, determined to ignore the feelings he aroused. Seated together, Carly noticed a slight resemblance between the brothers. Both had light brown hair, though Peter's had been recently cut and lacked the sun-kissed streaks of gold. They possessed similar profiles, but Mike's tanned skin glowed from time spent in the rugged outdoors. Peter possessed a refined polish, a veneer he'd worked hard to achieve. She appreciated both men's handsome looks... and refused to compare any further.

"Can we make it quick?" Peter asked. "I've got a brief to finish and file by nine tomorrow morning."

"Pete..."

"Sure," Carly said, cutting Mike off. He hadn't been around often enough to understand the demands of his brother's job. Having grown up the daughter of a prominent attorney, Carly did. "Humor me for a little while," she said and began to pull items from her bag.

Calendar, lists and pictures soon decorated the table. Despite Peter's token protests, Carly knew he realized that a few hours tonight would save them both a lot of aggravation in the future.

"See what I have to put up with?" Peter asked. She recognized the tinge of humor in his voice.

Mike glanced at Carly. "Life's rough, Pete. Next time a beautiful woman wants my undivided attention for a few hours, remind me to complain."

"Even if she wants to domesticate you?" Peter held up a glossy photo of a bride and groom.

The brothers shared a laugh, allowing Carly to see the bond that existed between them. One she hadn't truly believed in before now.

"In that case," Mike said, "I'd be on the first plane out of here."

Carly's stomach contracted painfully, a spasm she attributed to an aching emptiness and a sudden need... for food.

*   *   *

Mike yawned, glad the wedding plans were finally winding down.

"That's two P.M. Friday at the tuxedo place and ten A.M. Saturday at the florist?" Pete asked.

Carly glanced down at her appointment book and nodded. "No excuses, no delays." She pointedly raised her eyes and looked at her fiancé.

"As long as no surprises come up."

"They won't."

Mike closed the pizza box. Despite the presence of his brother and Carly, he'd eaten alone. For the better part of two hours, Carly and Peter had bargained their way through last minute wedding arrangements. If the couple sitting before him was to be believed, the perfect wedding involved little sentiment and a lot of details. The Carly Wexler he'd seen mooning over her favorite wedding band hours earlier had displayed more emotion than the one here tonight.

What had happened to the glimpse he'd gotten of the softhearted romantic? Around his brother, she was nowhere to be found.

"You'll be there or I'll compromise my principles and have my father cover your caseload himself." An angelic smile lit her features.

"Father?" Mike couldn't help but interrupt.

His brother glanced over. "Senior partner," he muttered. *A match made in professional heaven.* Mike nearly choked on a mouthful of soda.

Peter turned to Carly. "I'll be there," he promised.

"Then we're all set." She snapped her leather-bound diary closed.

"Definitely for the tuxedos, possibly for the flowers," Pete said in an obvious last-minute attempt to maneuver the plans to his advantage.

She lifted one eyebrow. Mike held his breath.

"Done," she said.

A woman who apparently knew when to accept compromise gracefully.

Peter stood. Carly followed, rising from her seat on

the floor. She stretched her arms above her head. Her round breasts lifted enticingly beneath the body-hugging material of her tank top. Mike's groin hardened, thrusting against the rough denim of his jeans. He swallowed a groan. A long night was about to get much longer.

"Time to let you get back to your work," she said to Peter.

His brother smiled. "A woman after my own heart." He placed one hand on the small of her back.

To his shock, Mike bit back a protest at the intimate contact. Throughout the evening, other than to ask Mike an occasional wedding-related question, Carly had ignored him. Having been the sole focus of her attention twice today, he couldn't help feeling slighted.

"Good job, you two," Mike said.

Startled, she whirled around and met his gaze. She brushed at her bangs. Her wide-eyed vulnerability hit him hard.

"Mike."

His name on her lips sounded incredibly right... despite the fact that his brother stood by her side.

"Good night." She ducked her head, brushing past him without another glance.

The vanilla scent he'd noticed earlier wrapped around him like a warm friend. "See you."

While Peter walked Carly to the door, Mike flipped channels on the television with the remote control. Their muffled voices and Carly's soft laugh drifted inside, commanding his attention. He swore and raised the volume a notch higher. Whether or not Peter kissed Carly was none of his concern. What those full lips would feel like was also none of his business.

With a guttural curse he'd picked up abroad, Mike turned off the television, rose and headed into the guest room. Better to face his nightmares than to eavesdrop on the two lovers saying good night.

TWO

Mike glanced around in disbelief. The tuxedo store couldn't possibly hold more than five people comfortably. Yet there had to be at least fifteen customers vying for the attention of two harassed salesmen. "I don't believe this," he muttered.

"I do."

Mike stood in the crowded store, too close to Carly, surrounded by her tantalizing scent. Whoever coined the term *best man* hadn't had him in mind. At this rate, his goal of getting in and out looked bleak. And though he'd enjoy a morning in her company, he didn't need the temptation. His brother wouldn't appreciate Mike's interest in his future wife.

"Looks like everyone wants to be a June bride," he said.

She rolled her eyes. "Did you get a good look around you? The girls can't be out of their teens and half of these guys have barely begun to shave. This is prom season, too." Folding her hands in her lap, she took a seat in a vacant chair in the corner.

Mike leaned against the wall beside her. "Since Peter's meeting us and he's typically late, I guess we'll have to wait anyway."

"True."

"Would you really have pulled rank on him?" Mike asked, seeking to understand this unlikely twosome. He knew that only a threat to Peter's career would keep his single-minded brother from getting lost in work and forgetting an appointment. Even for his own wedding.

"We'll never know, will we?" She sighed and glanced at her watch.

"He isn't late yet."

"I never said he was. I'm the one on a tight schedule today."

"Business or pleasure?"

"Both. I've got a late-afternoon deadline for my column and a four o'clock meeting."

"Pete mentioned something about an advice column and some kind of counseling." Mike glanced in Carly's direction, more than a little curious about the many facets of Carly Wexler.

"Mmm. I write a magazine column for teens and I'm also a high-school guidance counselor."

"Social worker?" he asked.

"Psychologist."

"Sounds like you're busy."

She shrugged. "It's seasonal. The fall is pretty hectic, but the summers are my own."

"A job with perks. I like that."

"Considering you're a world traveler, I don't doubt it," she said with a grin.

From across the room, a loud burst of male laughter was followed by distinctly feminine giggles. "What sort of advice do you give these kids?" Mike gestured in the direction of the carefree teens.

When was the last time he'd been *that* carefree? He wondered and immediately realized the incongruity of the question. He went out of his way to keep his life unencumbered by ties or commitments, yet lately he felt more burdened than ever before.

"They write in asking about how to deal with life. Friendship in some cases, love in others."

"And you answer with the voice of experience?"

"Hardly." She blushed a becoming shade of pink.

More like the voice of inexperience? Suddenly he wondered—about Carly, Pete, Carly and Pete—about a lot more than he had a right to know.

"I can't be late for that meeting." She, not so subtly, changed the topic.

"School appointment?" he asked.

She shook her head. "A publisher contacted me through the magazine. They'd like me to consider turning my columns into a self-help type of book."

"I'm impressed."

She waved away his compliment. "Good thing this shouldn't take long. Black double-breasted tuxedos, white shirt, wing-tipped shoes and black bow ties and cummerbunds. What could be simpler?"

"Or more boring."

She tilted her head backward and glared up at him. "What is that supposed to mean?" Fire flashed in her dark eyes, an unbelievable contrast to the controlled woman who'd sat with Peter and bartered over wedding arrangements.

The simmering passion intrigued him, made him want to dig deeper, beyond the exterior to the woman beneath. "Ever hear of color?" He deliberately baited her. "Or do you want the wedding party to resemble the Sunday *Times*?"

"Mike…"

"Sorry. Bridesmaids dresses bring in color, right? What would you pick? Pink?" He shook his head. "Too childish. There's yellow…"

"Mike."

"Peach."

"Mike."

"Or my personal favorite, purple." He eyed her intently. "Which is it?"

"White."

He groaned aloud. "Your choice?" he asked. *Not a*

chance in hell. Behind those rigid lists and schedules lurked a woman brimming with passion and fire. He'd bet his favorite camera on it.

More than once he'd ignited sparks in those expressive brown eyes. Sparks he'd yet to notice between Carly and her fiancé. His brother, he harshly reminded himself. "White," he muttered, shaking his head.

"Not my choice exactly. I wasn't sure. Peter wanted elegant, my mother wanted formal, so we…"

"Compromised," he finished for her. "It's a good thing you're so compliant."

"You make me sound like a well-behaved pet. Are you looking to start trouble?"

Looking for trouble? No. Looking for a glimpse of the untapped sensuality that sizzled beneath the conservative façade? Definitely. "Of course not," he said.

"Good. I just pick my battles carefully."

"I'll remember that. It's just…" He shook his head. "Never mind. None of my business."

Her eyes narrowed with distrust… and a slight spark? "What?" she asked through clenched teeth.

"This is your wedding, right?"

"Stupid question."

"Is it? For someone loaded down with wedding books and bridal pictures, you're giving up control of some major issues." He reached for her, covering her ice-cold hand with his warmer one. He gazed into her eyes. The spark erupted into a flame of unchecked desire.

His thumb brushed over her third finger, avoiding the large diamond ring that looked so out of place on her delicate hand. Traitorous desires consumed his body while conflicting emotions swirled inside his head. The pad of his thumb traced a pattern just above her knuckle, where her wedding band would sit. "Think about it," he murmured.

She shot him a look that could freeze hot coffee and wrenched her hand free from his.

"Miss Wexler?" a salesman greeted her. The rush of high-school students disappeared out the door, taking the loud laughs and boisterous shouts along with them. "Sorry to keep you waiting."

"That's okay." She stood, obviously grateful for the interruption.

"If you and your fiancé are ready to get started..." Mike remained standing against the wall and glanced at Carly.

She fingered her bangs, a nervous gesture he found awfully endearing. And sweet. The woman would never hold her own in a game of poker, but at least he'd never be left guessing about her true feelings.

"He's not my fiancé," she finally said.

"Future brother-in-law." The label grated. Mike

forced a smile and shook the other man's hand.

"Are we waiting for the groom?"

"No. We can start with the best man. Peter will be here soon," Carly said.

Wisely, Mike didn't touch that statement. Ten minutes later, he stood in front of a full-length mirror, decked out in formal attire. "Jacket's too tight," he said, rolling his bad shoulder to alleviate the discomfort. He'd deal with the bow-tie issue later.

"We have a tailor downstairs." The salesman brushed a hand across the back of the jacket.

*   *   *

Carly swallowed hard. The material rippled over Mike's broad shoulders. She clenched her hands into tight fists but the gesture didn't alleviate the need to touch him. Nor did it lessen the painful knot in her stomach.

The salesman continued to speak, drawing her attention back to tuxedos and tailoring. "Needs some alterations, but nothing major. If you folks will excuse me, I'll be right back."

Carly walked around Mike, scrutinizing the snug fit of the material and trying not to imagine the lean, hard body beneath the tailored clothing. "It suits you."

He shrugged. "I'm more comfortable in jeans and work boots."

He looked sexy in either. "More comfortable for the jungle, huh?" She took two steps backward. "What would you change... presuming the choice was yours?"

"For starters, this would have to go." He reached up and untied the black bow tie, tossing it onto the nearest chair. "Then this." He unbuttoned the conservative jacket and flung it aside. The black cummerbund followed.

Carly barely had time to assimilate his intent when he began to unbutton his shirt. "Now hang on a second."

He grinned but didn't stop removing his clothes. "You asked."

She watched in silence as he shed the shirt baring a tanned chest, muscular forearms and a flat stomach. Without warning, a wave of desire overcame common sense and her body reacted. The knot in her stomach tightened almost painfully, making her more aware of him than she had been before – if such a thing was possible.

He stood in front of her clad only in black trousers while she did her best to remain composed despite the rapid beating of her heart. "What next?" she managed to ask.

An irreverent gleam sparkled in his eyes, which appeared more golden than hazel, and held her in thrall.

"Don't answer that," she muttered.

"Close your eyes."

Carly did as he asked, hoping to find a respite from the newly awakened sexual feelings this man aroused. But her imagination failed to cooperate. Mike's tanned chest, well-muscled arms and overall powerful physique had been forever imprinted in her mind.

She heard the rustle of clothing and a few colorful curses before he finally spoke. "Open those beautiful eyes and tell me what you think."

Looking every inch the rebel, Mike's new outfit blatantly defied convention. His black European tuxedo jacket sported a shawl collar. In place of the old tuxedo shirt, he now wore a white collarless one, buttoned to the top. The lavender cummerbund distinguished him from the typical attorney look Carly was used to.

"I told you purple was my favorite." He grinned. "So what do you think?"

She opened her mouth to speak, but words wouldn't come. Considering the thoughts rampaging around her brain, perhaps that was just as well. A little wild, a little sexy and a lot she desired. Beyond that, Carly couldn't think at all.

"Your shirt's crooked." She walked up to him and stood on tiptoe. Her fingers gripped the front of the shirt. She drew a deep breath, only to find she'd made another mistake. His cologne, an enticing scent she'd recently come to know, seeped inside her.

She'd dreamed of this scent. Of him.

"Carly."

She glanced up, meeting his gaze. Now darkened by unmistakable need, his eyes turned a deeper shade of gold, and she felt drawn into the compelling depths. Unnerved, her fingers began to tremble.

He rested his warm hand on her waist. If he'd meant to steady her, his touch had the opposite effect and a tremor shot through her. A soft sigh escaped her lips.

He drew her close. Their bodies never connected, but something else did. His fingers tightened around her waist and the heat of his body wrapped her in warmth. Passion flared to life inside her. As if she could feel the imprint of his arousal against her skin, she ached for fulfillment. For him. Her hips jerked forward without her permission.

"Easy," he whispered, but his hold on her waist tightened.

In the back of her mind she heard the gentle tinkling of bells. Is this what she'd always feared? What she'd been so ingrained to distrust? Her father's love affair had destroyed so many lives. Carly had learned early that protestations of love couldn't be trusted and passion could only lead to disaster. But with Mike's arms wrapped firmly around her waist, the lessons of her parents' past seemed far away.

"Sorry I'm late, but a client showed up unexpectedly from the West Coast."

"Peter." With a startled gasp, Carly wrenched herself from Mike's embrace and turned to face her fiancé. "I was just…" She groped for an explanation and settled on the truth. "Crooked shirt," she said, gesturing toward Mike. Even as she spoke, she struggled to get hold of her emotions.

"I'm glad you started without me, but…" Peter's gaze darted to Mike. Seconds passed during which she held her breath before Peter turned back to face her. "I thought we agreed on conventional."

She exhaled, relieved that all seemed normal. Although she wondered if anything would ever be right again. But for now, with Peter focused on getting the "right look" and then heading back to the office, Carly realized that everything was truly fine. She was safe. For now.

She glanced at her fiancé. He studied his brother and shook his head. "With all the business associates who will be there, this won't work."

For the first time since planning her wedding, Carly vacillated—between the old need to make Peter happy and a sudden desire to please Mike. Between her old, compliant self and this unfamiliar woman with desires she didn't recognize.

"This was a joke, Pete." Mike grinned and tugged at the purple cummerbund. "I was just killing time."

Stark relief etched Peter's face. Carly turned away and mouthed a silent "thank you" in Mike's direction. His mouth tightened, but he nodded imperceptibly.

She inhaled and forced much needed air back into her lungs. Crisis averted, she thought, as Mike scooped up the original clothing and ducked inside the dressing room to change.

She ought to have felt relieved. So why did she feel so empty instead?

"That's it." Carly reached for the purse she'd hung over the side of the full-length mirror. She desperately needed fresh air and time alone.

"Don't forget dinner tomorrow night with your parents," Peter reminded her. "Your father wants to meet my brother." He turned to Mike. "And with the way your plans change, this might be his last chance for a while."

Carly caught her breath and pivoted on her heel. "I thought you were staying the month until the wedding." To her dismay, she hadn't kept the hint of panic from creeping into her voice.

Mike smiled, a warm, engaging smile, not the boyish grin he'd treated her to earlier. It was almost as if he knew she sought reassurance and wanted to relax her. But that was silly. "I am," he said with certainty. "I wouldn't miss this for anything."

"Oh." She swiped at her bangs. "Well then, I'd better get going. I can't afford to be late." She leaned forward and brushed a kiss on Peter's cheek.

She dared a brief glance at Mike. His penetrating gaze met hers. "'Bye," she whispered before heading for the door.

* * *

The tinkling of bells echoed long after she'd left. "Well," Mike said, turning toward his brother. "This trip home has been extremely interesting."

"How so?"

"I never thought I'd see the day you'd trade your freedom for a white picket fence."

Peter opened the top button on his white, starched shirt and tucked his paisley tie into his jacket pocket. "People change."

"Not that much. I thought you had one thing in mind: the fast track toward partnership."

Pete grinned. "I'm doing just that."

Which is what had Mike worried. "You're sure about this marriage?"

"Absolutely. Look, sometimes in life you compromise to get what you want. Carly and I get along well. She understands that business is important to me."

"She's something, all right," Mike muttered. He'd touched her and she'd nearly come apart in his arms. The memory still lingered, teasing his tenuous restraint. Even in passion, she radiated innocence, something lacking in his jaded life. "How'd you two meet?" he asked his brother.

"At a dinner honoring her father. She's been a good friend for the last few years."

Not an easy feat where his uptight self-absorbed brother was concerned. "I know it's none of my business, but is that a reason to get married?"

Pete sighed. "She's looking for a little stability, a happy home life, kids and her career. She'll have those things with me."

Mike watched his kid brother fidget the way he'd done after accidentally breaking the porch light with his baseball. Looking to protect him from their uncle's wrath, Mike had taken the blame and the punishment. And Peter had let him. Mike had a hunch that given the chance, Pete would still take the easy way out. "And what are you getting out of this... arrangement?"

"She's a sweet woman, Mike."

Tell me something I don't know. "And would her father being senior partner have something to do with this sudden urge to say 'I do?'"

"Doesn't hurt," he admitted. "Lately, new partnerships are rare. Even the most outstanding associates have been passed over. Things should return to normal with an economic upswing like this firm experienced last year."

"So Carly's added insurance." Mike couldn't suppress a groan.

"It's not like that." Pete gestured toward the door, and Mike followed his brother out to the street. The summer heat drifted up from the pavement. Mike broke into a sweat before they'd reached the corner.

"Do you love her?"

"No." Pete didn't hesitate before answering. "Not like you mean. But she's not in love with me either." He shrugged. "We have a mutual respect for one another, though, and that's more than a lot of married couples can say. I do care about her, Mike."

Not liking the matter-of-fact way Pete laid out what should have been emotional feelings, Mike clenched his fists at his sides. "You're something else, Pete."

"We're both adults and we understand each other."

So Carly had said. Mike didn't like the picture he'd gotten of this relationship, but their lives weren't his concern. As long as he repeated the mantra and believed it, he'd be fine. "Okay then, I'll drop the subject."

"I'll probably work late to make up for lost time this afternoon." Pete grinned. "So you're on your own for cold pizza. Unless…"

"I ate it this morning."

Pete groaned. Mike shrugged; he'd eaten a lot worse in much worse conditions. He pushed the encroaching memories aside. He glanced at his kid brother. "Hey, let me know how Carly's meeting with the publisher went."

Pete lifted an eyebrow. "What meeting?"

"Forget it. I must have misunderstood," Mike said, sensing that he'd understood perfectly. It was Carly and Pete who had yet to catch on.

"You'll be at dinner tomorrow?" his brother asked.

"To meet your boss?" His brother's future in-laws. Carly's parents. "Sure."

"Great. That means a lot." Peter turned toward the street and then back to Mike. "One more thing."

"What's that?"

"I'm training a new associate and my time is even more limited than before. If Carly needs any help planning or anything… would you be there?"

Mike hesitated, knowing time with Carly was dangerous for them both. Then again, his brother needed a favor, and Mike could use the distraction from dealing with his own unsettled life. Since his return, Mike had had too much free time to think. "No sweat."

"Thanks." Pete smiled and Mike knew he'd made the right decision. Time to discover whether these two were headed for disaster had nothing to do with his sudden agreement.

His brother hailed an empty cab. "I'm glad you're back."

"Me, too, Pete." But he hoped his brother didn't live to regret that sentiment.

However different Pete and Carly turned out to be, Mike had no right to interfere. The sooner Carly planned and executed this wedding, the better for everyone involved.

Especially Mike.

*   *   *

"A book contract. Carly Wexler, I am impressed."

"Glad you took a shot on a rookie?" Carly asked the editor of her column.

Juliette Parsons leaned forward in her seat, hands clasped in front of her on the age-worn desk. "I've been glad since day one."

"Me, too." And Carly wasn't just talking about her job. Since the day she'd been hired on as an intern at the magazine, Juliette had taken her under her wing.

Professionally, she treated Carly to stern lectures on proper writing technique. And Carly had turned to Juliette for personal advice far more than she'd ever allowed herself to turn to her own mother.

She sat down on the futon couch in Juliette's office. Among her other qualities, Juliette was a bit of an eccentric. Juliette pressed the intercom on her phone. "Herbal tea, Stacey. Two, please." Then she joined Carly on the couch. "So tell me what Peter said."

Carly bit down on her lip. "About what?"

Her friend's blue eyes opened wide. "You haven't told him?"

"I thought I'd surprise him with the news."

"Ahh. He must be on pins and needles waiting to hear. If he can tear himself away from his office," Juliette muttered almost under her breath.

"I heard that."

"You were supposed to." She pulled her long hair back and twisted it into a bun at the base of her neck. "But he is waiting to hear?"

"Umm... I wanted to keep the news to myself in case it fell through."

"In that case, who would have comforted you if you were down?"

Mike. Carly pushed the traitorous thought aside. She had no business thinking of Peter's brother that way.

"I'd have confided in Peter." Eventually. If he had time. She shook her head, surprised at how disloyal she seemed to have become in such a short time. Peter deserved better from the woman he was going to marry.

"Good." Juliette patted her hand. "If you're looking to surprise him, I suppose he must be improving in the stuffy department."

Carly sighed. "Juliette, you know he has to work hard. He cares; he just doesn't show it the way Armando does." She paused, thinking about Juliette's ardent and amorous lover. "Come to think of it, no one shows it the way Armando does."

"It's the Latin in him." Juliette grinned. "Sexy men make sensual, lasting lovers. I should know. We've been together for ten years."

Carly rolled her eyes. They'd had this conversation too many times to count. "What a man's like in bed is no reflection on whether a couple has a lasting future."

Juliette raised a knowing eyebrow. "How would you know?"

Carly sighed. "So we haven't slept together… it doesn't mean we don't have staying power."

"What I don't get is the *why*. You're marrying him. Seems to me you ought to want him, too."

She twisted uncomfortably in her seat. Not from the topic of conversation, because she and Juliette could talk about anything, but because of the deadly accuracy of her friend's point. She cared about Peter, but she didn't much care that they hadn't consummated their relationship. The desire wasn't all-consuming and strong… which was a large part of the reason she wanted to marry him. He was safe. Safe from passion, safe from her family's past. And she loved him for that.

"There's time, Juliette."

Her friend leaned forward. "Not if you're marrying for the wrong reasons. Then you'll find out too late that you made a mistake."

"Are you saying my marriage to Peter is wrong?" Carly tensed, almost afraid to hear the answer.

"Of course not. Only you would know that. I just worry about you."

"Well, don't, because there's no problem." A knock on the door prevented Carly from following up on that statement. A good thing, since she didn't feel as secure as she sounded. After Juliette's assistant left the tea and two bone-china cups on a table, Juliette poured, then slid Carly's cup across the glass table.

"Chamomile?" Carly asked, glancing at the light amber-colored liquid.

"This week's blend is lavender and patchouli. It will soothe your nerves, and some believe it acts as an aphrodisiac. But only you will know whether that is true."

She eyed Juliette doubtfully.

The older woman shrugged. "What do you have to lose? Drink up and maybe you'll be the one surprised tonight."

"Anything is possible," Carly murmured. She lifted the cup and took a hefty sip.

*   *   *

Feeling light-headed and giddy, Carly packed the dinner she had ordered from Peter's favorite gourmet restaurant. She stopped at the liquor store across the street from his office. On a whim, she splurged and bought the most expensive brand of champagne the small shop carried. Maybe Juliette was right and tonight would be a special one for her and Peter.

Clutching the bottle under her arm, she waved at the same rotund security guard who'd held the night shift since she was in her teens. He'd seen her grow up and no longer required her to sign in or call after hours.

At eight P.M. the reception area was empty, and Carly wound her way back to the large conference room at the end of a long hall. Hushed voices and a feminine laugh rang out in the quiet office. She rounded the corner and stopped in the doorway. She'd expected to find Peter and one or more of his colleagues, hard at work, preparing for an important closing in the morning.

Instead she found Peter and a very feminine, very young associate sharing a laugh over a large pizza. The woman appeared relaxed, her stockinged feet perched on a chair beside Peter's. And Carly's meticulously neat fiancé had loosened his tie and tucked the end inside his shirt, presumably to avoid stains. He'd rolled up his sleeves and leaned back, feet propped, in a comfortable-looking chair. Unopened legal-size folders sat in a stack on the conference table. From the look of things, they'd remain unopened for a while.

Though she'd had second thoughts about stopping by unannounced, Carly was suddenly glad she had. Their relationship could obviously benefit from added spice and her surprise would be a great start.

"Excuse me." Carly cleared her throat, "I hope I'm not interrupting."

Startled, Peter's feet hit the floor with a thud. "Carly."

"Last time I looked."

He shot her a curious glance. The casual banter that came so naturally around Mike fell flat with Peter.

"This is a surprise," he said.

"Good or bad?"

His eyebrows creased in confusion. "Neither. It just is."

Carly forced herself to remain composed. Not an easy task while standing in the doorway holding a picnic basket in one hand and a bottle of bubbly in the other, spouting bad jokes and feeling ridiculously out of place.

Peter hadn't yet noticed her packages.

"Is this your fiancé?" The petite brunette rose from her seat, turning to face Carly.

"Yes. Roger's daughter." He gestured between the two women. "Carly Wexler, Regina Grey."

"Nice to meet you," Carly said.

"Same here. I've heard a lot about you."

I wish I could say the same. "All good, I hope."

"All fathers have nothing but wonderful things to say about their daughters." Regina smiled and took a long sip of bottled water. "And of course," she continued, "Peter speaks highly of you as well."

"Of course." Away from the office, Peter was preoccupied with work. At the office, he was preoccupied with Carly. Yeah, right. This pint-sized barracuda certainly didn't need any courtroom training in how to go for the jugular.

Peter wrapped one arm around Carly's shoulders. "You know I enjoy seeing you, but two surprises in one week?"

"Shocking, I know. Next time I'll call." She could no longer keep the hurt out of her voice.

"That's not what I meant, but this is unexpected. What are you doing here?"

The compulsion to share her news with Peter had evaporated as quickly as it had come. "Nothing important. I thought I'd bring dinner." She raised her arms to show him her bag of goodies.

"Oh. Well. Uh, we've already…" He stammered and flushed a deep crimson.

"Eaten. I can see that. Don't worry. You two are busy, so I'll be going."

Peter brushed a strand of hair off her cheek. "After the florist on Saturday, we'll do wedding bands. How's that?"

She plastered a smile on her face. "Sounds great." But for some reason, this didn't feel like a compromise she'd won. In fact, his gesture seemed out of place, like that of a man who'd bought his wife flowers to assuage his guilt over an affair. She ought to know. She'd seen her father exhibit those signs often enough, growing up.

With his hand on the small of her back, Peter guided her out and toward the bank of elevators. Not five minutes after she'd arrived, Carly took the same elevator down with the same full picnic basket and expensive bottle of champagne in her hands. Some surprises backfired, she thought. And this had been one of them.

THREE

With mellow jazz music playing on the stereo, Carly settled herself on a plush pillow in front of her cocktail table. She unpacked the gourmet meal and uncorked the bottle of champagne.

She poured champagne into a wineglass and lifted it in the air. "Congratulations," she muttered and downed the bubbly wine. She poured some more and enjoyed the bubbles as they tickled their way down her throat. No matter how lousy she felt, at least the expensive champagne wouldn't go to waste.

When the doorbell rang the first time, she ignored the sound. The second chime was a more prolonged spurt. "Go away. This isn't an open party."

At the sound of the third ring, she picked up a drumstick and padded barefoot across the hardwood floor. She peered through the peephole and cursed the heavens. How could she possibly forget about this man if he showed up on her doorstep uninvited?

Drawing a deep breath, she opened the door. "Did you smell the chicken all the way uptown?" she asked.

"Cute."

That crooked grin did funny things to her heart.

"Aren't you going to invite me in?" he asked.

She bowed and waved Mike into her small apartment. The haven where she was safe from everyone and everything. Including her own feelings. *But no more.*

She shut the door behind him and followed him inside. He glanced around the living room and frowned. "You shouldn't be drinking alone."

"I'm not, I'm celebrating."

"By yourself?"

"It doesn't take two to celebrate, Mike."

He grinned. "No, but it's a heck of a lot more fun."

At his deliberate innuendo, she felt the heat rise to her face.

"You made a deal with the publishers?" The genuine excitement in his voice brought her earlier rush of adrenaline back full force.

She nodded, pleased with herself, proud of what she'd accomplished and suddenly not ashamed to show it. "Yup. A good deal, too."

"Hey!" Before she knew what hit her, he'd swept her into his arms and twirled her around the floor. His body felt warm and hard against her breasts.

"That's great."

As he lowered her to the floor, the slight bulge in

his pants caused a quickening in her stomach. Apparently Juliette's aphrodisiac worked all right... with the wrong brother. Carly stepped back to avoid further contact.

"How about another glass so I can share the celebration?"

Using the time to catch her breath, Carly walked into the kitchen and returned with a second wineglass. She grinned. "Only the finest."

"I'm used to drinking out of bottles and cans. Anything else is paradise."

"Peter said something about you being a photojournalist?"

"I was," Mike said.

"And now you're...?"

"On vacation," he said smoothly. He glanced around the room and chose a reclining chair in the corner. It rocked slightly under his weight and he laughed. "I love these things."

She smiled. "Me, too."

"So much more comfortable than that hard leather thing Pete calls a couch."

Carly's smile faded and he regretted whatever he'd said to cause the change.

"I see. Talking about work is off-limits?" She pushed the topic away from herself and back to him.

"Not if there's something you really want to

know."

"What subjects have you covered recently?"

"This and that," he said, unwilling to delve deeper into his most current assignment. Even for Carly.

"Can't you be more specific?"

I'd prefer not to. "I cover hard news. I don't dig around in celebrity trash cans." He forced a grin.

She smiled in understanding. Her brown eyes met his. A man could drown in the compassion he saw there. "I'd like to see your work sometime," she said.

"My pleasure." That he wanted to share his private photos with Carly gave him some indication of his level of involvement. More than was prudent he knew. For a man who avoided emotional entanglements, the revelation stunned him.

He forced himself to think of his brother and suppressed a groan. "After you left this afternoon, I spoke with Pete."

"And?"

"Since he'll be busy training a new associate, I'm at your disposal for any wedding-related things you need." *Or anything else, for that matter.*

"Training. Is that what they call it these days?"

"What?"

"See this?" Her arm swept the table loaded with food that smelled amazing. Between the canned food he'd eaten overseas and the takeout he'd feasted on since his return, Carly's table looked like manna from heaven.

So did she. A silky lemon yellow pajama set—pants and a long-sleeved top—draped across her soft curves and smooth skin. The material rustled as she crossed the room.

"Chicken, gourmet salads, caviar and assorted desserts. All your brother's favorites."

He glanced from the food to her stricken expression. "He stood you up?" That thought was as sickening to him as the thought of Carly greeting his brother dressed for bed.

"No, that would have hurt," she admitted. "He wasn't at fault; I was. I broke the ultimate taboo."

Her cheeks burned with color and a range of emotion flared in her eyes. She was, Mike decided, either angry or on her way toward drunk. He couldn't determine which. He glanced at the bottle, but the deep green obscured the level of the liquid inside.

He turned back to Carly. "And what was that?" he asked.

"I showed up, unexpectedly, dinner in hand for my overworked fiancé."

"He ignored you for *work*?" *The selfish bastard.* Mike stood, crossing the room until he was close enough to breathe the intoxicating scent of vanilla. Who needed champagne when a man could get drunk on this?

"Nope. Guess again."

He rubbed his forehead, wondering what his moron brother, who cared about but didn't love Carly, had done now. "Was he angry you surprised him?"

"Nope. Guess again." A smile quirked around the edges of her mouth. "Three strikes and you're out."

Mike tossed his hands in the air in a gesture of defeat. "I give up. What happened?" If his brother had hurt her, Mike would ring his stuffy neck.

"He was already eating." She paced the floor. Her hips swayed beneath the opaque material.

He already knew he could span her waist with his bare hands. "And?"

"And laughing." She whirled around to face him. "Did you ever hear anything so ridiculous? Peter was laughing with that associate *in training*—who, by the way, needs as much training as Flipper."

Mike walked up beside her and placed a comforting hand on her shoulder. "Was he doing anything... wrong?"

She shook her head slowly from side to side.

"Anything... unethical maybe?"

Again, she shook her head. "But he laughed." She leaned against a pink marbleized wall and sighed. "He never laughs with me."

The admission cost her, Mike could tell. She looked up at him, her eyes bright with unshed tears.

"And I can't remember the last time I laughed with him."

"Oh, sweetheart." *I could have told you that.*

He placed a hand around her waist, ignoring how easily she fit her body to his, how soft and right she felt in his arms, and led her to the oversized pillow on the floor.

Seating himself next to her, Mike took her hand in his. "If you think you're making a mistake, now's the time…"

"No!" Carly jerked her hand back and rubbed it against the silk pants. "I didn't say that. It's just that with planning the wedding, things have been tense. His work, my work… you know how it is."

Oh, yeah. He knew. And he had a strange feeling she did, too. So why push so hard for something that wasn't right? That would only make her unhappy for the next fifty or so years? And why didn't his intelligent brother, who'd attended college and law school on scholarships, see the truth?

Mike sighed, reminding himself that he'd be back touring the world in no time and Carly's pain would be a distant memory. Or would it?

"Okay, then. Let's eat and help you plan. After all, you've only got three weeks left until the big day."

"Later. Right now I just want to relax." She busied herself loading up two plates with food, setting one down in front of Mike and refilling the champagne glasses.

For the next hour, he amused her with tales about his less than glamorous assignments, some of the more squalid places he'd slept and the interesting people he'd met along the way. Though he hoped the stories would bring back a wave of nostalgia for the life he'd left behind, all he felt was an aching emptiness for all he lacked—and that, more than anything else, made him nervous.

He helped Carly clean up her living room and put the half-full bottle of champagne into the fridge. Since she'd had one glass and he'd shared a fair amount himself, he realized Carly's earlier fit hadn't been made while drunk. It had been made while hurt and angry at his insensitive brother. Mike's hands clenched into fists at his sides.

While she replaced what appeared to be volumes of magazines on top of her cocktail table, Mike indulged his curiosity. He examined the wall of bookshelves, astounded at the number of self-help books crammed into the narrow space. Then he appraised the apartment with a photographer's eye. Moonlight filtered in through a bay window, catching vibrant colors in its wayward beams. The oversized recliner matched the comfortable sofa and picked up the pale pink shade on the walls.

Organization offset by plush comfort. Everything said *touch me*. Nothing had the stark, hands-off feeling of Pete's apartment, a place where Mike slept but had yet to feel at home. That he did here, didn't surprise him. Shook him up some, but what was one more punch in the gut when everything around him seemed to be falling apart?

His career—hell, his life for that matter—was in shambles. This engagement between two polar opposites shouldn't have any effect on him, yet he cared for both people involved... one of whom he'd known for one week. In three weeks he'd be her brother-in-law.

"Mike?"

Her light touch on his arm startled him. "Yeah?"

"Are you okay? You seem a little... I don't know. Out there."

He smiled. "I'm fine. And you ought to get some sleep."

She nodded, watching him with those deep brown eyes as he headed for the door. He turned back to find her close behind him. Her scented perfume drifted around him, causing his body to stir in an unbrotherly way. Captured in a sensual haze, he remembered the moment she'd fixed his cummerbund, when her body had jerked against him. His hands had itched to cup her breasts, to pull her close and bury himself deep inside her. If not for the fact that they'd been in a public place, he would have.

No such restraints bound him now... but too many others did. They'd come too damn close. "Hell," he muttered. He didn't need this aggravation. Whatever happened to brotherly devotion? To loyalty?

He thought of Pete, who counted on this woman for all the wrong reasons. The only right one was love, something his sibling had instantly discounted. This entire situation was a mess Mike could do without. If he was smart, he'd forget he'd ever met Carly Wexler.

He looked into those bottomless eyes. He could no more forget her than he could fail to respond to the innocence in her gaze. Without conscious thought, he fingered her bangs. The strands felt like fine silk. He bent down and brushed his mouth across hers.

She tasted unique, sweet with a hint of champagne. His lips lingered for a second, pulling back before he lost control. "Take care, Carly."

Forcing his feet to move, he turned and walked out without looking back.

*　　*　　*

With Mike gone, the apartment felt more like a lonely prison. She left the living room and headed for the safety of her bedroom. The one place in the small apartment Mike hadn't marked with his presence.

She paused at the foot of her bed and glanced at the newspaper article she'd been reading earlier. *Looking for Mr. Right. Is Your Man the Man for You?* She shouldn't have to wonder, and until the arrival of Peter's wandering brother, she never had.

With Peter she'd looked forward to an uncomplicated, comfortable relationship. *Comfortable* being the important word. They shared the same ideals. Marriage, family and career, if not necessarily in that order. They shared the same circle of friends, courtesy of his working for her father. And though he was an attorney like Roger Wexler, she'd trusted that when he said he had to work late, she'd find him at the office, not in another woman's bed.

Regina's face came to mind and Carly pushed it aside. People who worked together often bonded. How could they not, with the amount of hours they spent together? But she and Peter shared something more important. The comfort factor she found so important had always been there, and *that* was something she could count on, and so could he.

She closed her eyes, but instead of her fiancé, Mike's deep laugh, handsome face and well-honed body filled her mind. She touched her lips with her fingers. They tingled at the thought of Mike's mouth on hers. Disgust filled her.

She'd come so close…

Close to following in her father's footsteps.

How could she be so careless as to forget that passion destroys? She picked up the page and gazed at the article in her hand. No, Carly thought. She didn't need to find Mr. Right. She already had.

For a brief second the sparkling diamond ring caught her eye. She was engaged to the right man. She had to be. With a sigh, she crumpled the article into a ball and arced it toward the center of the room.

Life was filled with compromise. So Peter wasn't perfect. Neither was she. In an imperfect world, one made the best choices possible and honored one's commitments. Unlike her father, Carly intended to live by those rules. Intense passion burned itself out fast. It meant little when compared to a lifetime.

Putting Mike out of her mind wouldn't be easy, but it was necessary. Yet how could she do that with him helping her out at every turn, being so damn nice, when Peter all but ignored her, and he was just being... Mike.

*　*　*

Mike stretched his arms over his head. He'd hit the sack early, but the hours he'd spent tossing and turning in bed didn't count. He hadn't slept much or well and all because of Carly. And that told him that he had too much free time on his hands. So he decided to make some inquiries.

By late afternoon, he'd not only called in a few favors and arranged a Saturday afternoon meeting with the editor of the local paper, but he'd also secured the job. The guy was impressed with Mike's credentials and portfolio of shots. He was as pleased to have Mike on board as Mike was to have a temporary job to occupy his free time.

Mike had never been one to sit idle while the rest of the world passed him by. On the plane ride home, he'd told himself that a temporary position would keep him from thinking too much, yet allow him time to sort out his future. His ultimate return had never been in question... he just wasn't ready. Now, with the unexpected Peter and Carly saga, Mike felt more compelled than ever to stick around. The thought of Carly and his brother together turned his usually strong stomach.

So he was staying, at least, for a while. He'd make his own hours, giving him time to learn more about his brother's soon-to-be wife. That thought, alone, should have sent him running for the first flight out of New York. Anywhere USA would work just fine. Unfortunately, even the next town over would lack the presence of the bright lights and fast pace of New York. Lack the presence of one dark-eyed beauty who'd been haunting his dreams with more frequency than back-biting bullets and screaming children.

* * *

Carly approached the wedding band issue with bright-eyed optimism. After all, two people sharing a life together wanted to make each other happy. Standing in front of the jewelry store, it was hard not to remember her first meeting with Mike. But she pushed the memory aside. No point in looking to the past when she had a future to build.

She peeked into the window and the cramping in her stomach eased when she saw her favorite rings were still there. She placed a hand on Peter's elbow. "Look," she whispered, pointing to the simple wedding bands she'd chosen with Mike.

"They are nice," he said. It sounded like a reluctant concession drawn from deep inside him. "But how would a ring like that look?" he asked, and she knew she was right.

"Beautiful?"

"Anything would look lovely on you. But people would think I couldn't afford to get you something special."

"Those are special." She grit her teeth while she spoke. She knew she was being obtuse. For the first time, she didn't care.

He sighed. "Perhaps I didn't explain that correct-

ly." He paused. "I'd like something with more...
presence." Silence followed while he perused the
window display. He tapped the glass thoughtfully.
"Something understated but designed to impress."

"Like those?" Her voice lost any enthusiasm at all,
but her fiancé, too caught up in his own needs, failed
to notice.

"No... like... those!"

Carly cringed at Peter's preference, a ring that
glittered with diamonds and would overpower her
small hand.

*For someone loaded down with wedding books and bridal
pictures, you're giving up control of some major issues.* Had
Mike been right? Was she too compliant? She shook
her head. No! Peter's reasons for wanting the more
obvious rings had to do with his status and need to
impress his colleagues. She understood. Mike didn't.

Besides, what did the world traveler, a man incapable of sticking around longer than the next
assignment, know about commitment anyway?

But she and Peter did have conflicting desires.
That much was true. She wanted the chance to
convince Peter that commitment meant more to her
than flashy rings and making a statement. That
sentiment counted more than points scored with his
colleagues.

As he grabbed her hand and pulled her into the

store, Carly was determined to do just that.

*　　*　　*

"So did you two compromise on wedding bands today?" Mike took a sip of his Scotch and soda, ignoring Carly's furious glare. He wondered from which parent she'd inherited those expressive eyes, then realized he'd find out soon enough.

"We chose the perfect rings," his brother said, then turned toward the bar. "I'll have the same and a glass of white wine for the lady."

"Let me guess," Mike said. "Two-toned platinum and gold by chance?"

"Actually…" Peter began.

"I didn't like them as much once I saw them a second time. Peter picked out a pair that suited us much better," Carly said, a forced smile on her lips.

Sure he did, sweetheart. More likely her good nature had gotten lost in his brother's well-meaning but overwhelming need to impress others. "Well, good. Because I'd hate to see a bride getting married with a wedding band she didn't love. One she'd have to wear the rest of her life. That she'd compromised on…"

"We get the picture," she said through clenched teeth. "If you'll both excuse me, I see some friends I'd like to say hello to." She gave Peter a brief kiss on the cheek. A chaste kiss more suited to a friend of the family than her fiancé. What was it with these two? Mike wondered, and not for the first time.

"We'll be here," Peter said.

Mike merely shook his head, watching as Carly wound her way through the crowded club. Her black dress was simple yet clung to every curve. He gulped a mouthful of Scotch.

Peter rested one elbow on the bar. "Thanks for making it tonight. Wexler and Greene is a large firm, but they make it a policy to get to know their associates well."

Mike suppressed a groan. "Marriage isn't the same as a merger, Pete. Work probably has nothing to do with this dinner. You're marrying the man's daughter, for heaven's sake."

"What? You think by meeting you, he's checking me out?"

Mike shrugged. "Could be. Maybe he's checking out the family, making sure Carly's not getting stuck with the wrong sort of people." He slapped his brother on the back. "At least you're safe there. Two orphans with no family to speak of. I'd say the man doesn't have much to concern himself with. How 'bout you?"

A wry smile touched Peter's lips. "True. So long as you're on your best behavior, I'll have no problem. And maybe the partnership will follow."

"That's what I love about you, Pete."

"What's that?"

"Nothing gets in the way of work."

"Of course not."

The insult obviously went over his brother's head, but what could be expected from a man who took most things literally and only work seriously?

"Anyhow, I doubt Roger would check me out for Carly's sake. Those two aren't particularly close."

Mike grabbed a handful of peanuts from a dish on the bar. "Why not?"

"Who knows? They do the father-daughter thing, but it's mostly for show." Peter rubbed his forehead with one hand. Finally, he lifted his shoulders. "If Roger has any interest in me at all, it must be professional."

Mike remained silent. The dynamics at work in these relationships went way beyond anything he'd seen before. He doubted things were as simple as Peter made them out to be. But he knew for sure Pete was oblivious to anything that concerned Carly and her family unless it affected his career.

If Mike was smart, he'd take his cue from his self-centered brother. He downed the rest of his drink, but knowing where Carly was concerned, he was anything but smart.

* * *

A small band played in the corner of the darkened dining room. Mirrors lined the walls and reflected light gave the impression of a larger room than the otherwise intimate atmosphere implied. With Carly beside him, Mike found relaxing all but impossible. The sweet scent of her perfume had him on edge, shifting uncomfortably in his seat. More than once, he'd jolted himself out of a sensual daydream that had her writhing with passion beneath him.

With her father on his left side and his brother seated to her right, fantasies involving Carly Wexler were not only disrespectful, but downright wrong. Peter, oblivious to everything, had involved Anne Wexler in a discussion about attorneys and their wives.

Those beautiful brown eyes had come from Anne, Mike realized, but Carly possessed an inner warmth. She seemed almost to glow from within. Dressed in an ice blue chiffon gown, her mother appeared cool and aloof. Although friendly, she lacked her daughter's special sparkle, the elusive something that drew Mike so deeply.

"Mike," Roger said, "Peter tells me you've been out of the country on assignment until recently."

Mike nodded. "The Middle East," he said by way of clarification. A place and a subject he was in no mood to revisit. "But I wouldn't miss my brother's wedding," he said, returning to a topic he found more interesting.

"I can hardly believe it's almost time to walk my only daughter down the aisle."

Carly shifted, her bare leg brushing his for a split second before she realized and jerked away. Mike suppressed a grin and tried to concentrate on her father's musings.

Beside him, she lifted a glass of water and brought it to her lips.

"It seems like only yesterday she was a teenager, and now she's all grown up." The older man sighed wistfully.

"It happens, sir."

"I really miss those days."

The glass slipped from Carly's hand. Mike caught and steadied the crystal goblet before more than a few drops of water splattered onto the plate.

"Carly?"

"I'm fine."

He doubted it. "No harm done," he murmured. Beneath the table, he squeezed her hand in a token gesture of comfort before reaching to wipe the small mess.

"Thanks," she whispered. One look at her ashen face had him questioning the depth of this father-daughter relationship. She wrung the linen napkin between her hands. Peter had been mistaken. Carly cared... too much.

No one except Mike appeared to notice her discomfort. He waited until they'd all ordered before turning to his brother. "Do you mind if I dance with your future wife?" Before getting that close to Carly, Mike needed to cement their status in his mind.

Peter leaned back in his chair and smiled. "My pleasure. I'll just..."

"Spend time discussing business," Mike finished for him. As if there was any other ending to the sentence, Mike thought. "Okay, then." He pushed back his chair and rose from his seat.

"May I?" He extended his hand toward Carly.

If ever someone needed to get away from friends, family and all-around stress, Carly did. And he wanted to be her salvation, if only for the night. No one, including her parents or her fiancé, had realized how shaken she was. Another telling sign, he thought.

"I don't think a dance is such a good idea." She glanced around her for confirmation, but everyone else was already engrossed in conversation.

She looked at his outstretched hand. With the slightest hesitation, she put her napkin down on the table and rose from her seat, placing her warm hand in his.

Mike's insides did a one-eighty. For a man who faced danger daily while on assignment without flinching, this sudden kick of adrenaline was a warning. Sexual chemistry was one thing. Caring another.

*   *   *

Carly followed Mike, unable to understand how he'd read her so well. He'd sensed her discomfort and offered her a chance to compose herself away from prying eyes. She already knew a dangerous attraction raced between them. She didn't need or want an emotional connection with him as well.

As they approached the dance floor, Carly felt as though she were stepping over an imaginary boundary, crossing a path that would lead to nothing but disaster if she wasn't careful. Yet with each step away from the table and toward Mike, her mood lightened. His grip tightened on her hand, prompting hers to do the same.

The floor was neither crowded, nor were they the only couple dancing. There was enough room for them to maneuver comfortably without feeling crushed, yet enough people surrounding them to offer her the illusion of being safe in Mike's arms. He drew her close, slipping his arm around her back while still keeping a respectable space between them. She appreciated his discretion, and yet there was nothing respectable about her feelings for Mike.

"Was my SOS that obvious?" she asked.

"Only to someone paying attention," he said, implying what she'd already realized on her own.

Though she ought to jump to her fiancé's defense, she was too tired to make the effort. She glanced at Mike and smiled. "Well, thank you, sir."

"No problem, ma'am," he drawled.

She tilted her head back in time to catch his lopsided grin and couldn't contain the impish smile he inspired in return. When silence descended, she let herself drift in time to the music. She laid one hand on his shoulder, idly moving her fingers along his jacket, feeling the broad planes of his chest and the ripple of muscle beneath the material. She heard his deep breath at the same time he captured her hand in his, intertwining their fingers.

Embarrassed, she searched for a neutral topic.

"After all your travels, family dinners must bore you to tears."

"You'd be surprised." His gaze roamed over her face before he captured the back of her head in his strong hand and settled her head against his chest. But he kept her wandering hand wrapped in his, close to his heart.

The song changed to a slow, romantic ballad. As the lights dimmed, more couples joined them on the dance floor, forcing Mike's body closer. The rasp of material as his jacket brushed her linen dress sounded unnaturally loud in her ears.

She glanced up to find his golden eyes smoldering with unspoken need. For Carly, the world had shrunk in size, to two people dancing in near twilight, alone with each other.

When she drew a deep breath, she was enveloped by the essence of Mike. She closed her eyes and rested her head against his shoulder, feeling like she'd come home. Without warning, the music shifted again, this time to a 1970s' pop song. Carly was bumped from behind, pushed against Mike... and discovered he desired her much the same way she wanted him. The proof of something she'd spent the last week alternately denying and forcing out of her mind sent her reeling. She backed off immediately.

"Carly, wait."

She turned. "Please don't say anything."

"But…"

"Not a single word." She placed one finger over his lips, and then jerked back as if she'd touched a live wire. With a single touch or a heated glance, the man caused her nerve endings to tingle and her entire body to vibrate in a way that was both new and familiar at the same time.

She clenched her fists to keep from trembling. "I'm going back to the table before anyone misses us."

He opened his mouth to speak.

"Now, please." She cut him off, the entreaty in her voice plain.

*   *   *

Mike, powerless to deny this woman anything, turned and followed her back to the table. His body still burned from a simple dance.

He held Carly's chair before lowering himself into his seat beside her. He had to bite back a curse as his brother covered her hand with his.

"That's the best news I've heard in months." Peter beamed with pleasure, more honest emotion than Mike had seen since his return.

"What's that?" Carly asked. She laid a hand on Peter's arm. Mike tensed, but said nothing.

"Partnership decisions have been moved up," Roger said. "We've seen a boost in almost every department and want to make up for the last few years. We'll make final decisions in about a week and a half."

"That's great news, Pete." Mike knew his brother lived and breathed little else but work. This turn of events ought to make him ecstatic.

"Carly?" Anne looked at her daughter. Obviously she expected some reaction from the soon-to-be wife of an attorney and almost partner.

"Great," Carly echoed.

Sincere but flat. Anne didn't appear to notice. Mike did.

"Well, with that settled…" Anne smiled and then cleared her throat. "I mean almost settled. What's going on with the wedding details? Are you all set?"

Carly nodded. "Pretty much." She leaned closer to Mike to allow the waiter room to maneuver.

Caesar salad had always been Mike's favorite, and when everyone had been served, he picked up his fork.

"All that's left is the final fitting on my dress."

Mike's appetite disappeared. Watching as Carly moved one leaf around the plate, he surmised that she wasn't any hungrier than he.

"I'll be glad to go with you," Anne said, hope shining in her eyes. "After all, it isn't every day your daughter gets married."

Whatever Mike's first impressions of Anne Wexler, they were obviously as false as the shield she hid behind. It was obvious, now, that she loved her daughter but feared being rejected.

"No, thanks, Mom. I don't need your help. I've got a million errands to run and last-minute appointments before the high school graduation."

"All of which have nothing to do with me. I want to be there. Just name the time."

Carly raised her eyes from her dish and glanced toward her mother. "I'll probably just drop by the bridal shop during lunch on Friday."

"Friday's the Bar Association luncheon honoring your father." Disappointment radiated from Anne in waves.

"I know, and I can handle this alone. After all, the dress is picked. It's just a final fitting."

"But every bride needs someone there for them." Anne paused. "Your bridesmaids?" she asked hopefully.

"Are coming from out of town, you know that. And Juliette has a business lunch."

Anne turned toward her husband, her intention clear.

"No! You belong with Dad. I can deal with this alone. I'm fine, Mom."

Mike couldn't take it anymore. For either of them. "If you need a second opinion, I could help out." He draped an arm over Carly's chair and leaned back. "I might enjoy it," he said with a grin.

Peter looked up from his conversation with Roger. "Not a bad idea, Carly. At least you'd have someone there... you know, for moral support."

"I don't need..."

"Sure you do," Pete insisted. "You've handled all this on your own, planned everything, picked everything."

She raised a napkin to those luscious lips. "Not

quite everything," she muttered, then lowered the napkin back to her lap.

Mike shifted his wrist and tapped her on the shoulder. "I don't mind."

"We can't," she said. "It's bad luck or something."

He roared with laughter. "Why would you say that?"

"It's not like he's the groom," Pete said, joining Mike for a laugh.

Suddenly, Mike didn't find the subject all that amusing. "If you want me, I'm available," he said, suppressing the nudging guilt that threatened whenever he even thought about Carly.

Mike loved his brother. For Peter, Mike felt a kinship born of childhood struggles. For Carly, Mike felt... something stronger than he could put into words. But regardless of Peter's faults or reasons for this engagement, Mike's interest in his brother's fiancé was low.

If he allowed Carly to come between them, he would lose the only family he had left. And so would Pete. For that reason alone, Mike was determined to keep a safe distance from Carly from here on in. With all the self-control that had gotten him the perfect picture numerous times, that shouldn't be too difficult. But his conflicting desires just might tear him apart.

"Carly?" Peter laid a hand on her bare arm. Mike

clenched his teeth in response.

"Okay," she said, glancing at Mike. "I'd appreciate it."

"Mike?" Peter glanced at him, one eyebrow lifted, waiting for an answer.

"Sure." He'd help her. He'd help Pete. But at what cost? And to whom?

FOUR

Operating under the assumption that busy minds didn't have time to think, Carly awoke early and spent the morning tackling belated spring cleaning and ignoring the persistent ring of her cell phone. Unfortunately, she couldn't do the same thing with the doorbell.

She wiped her dusty hands on her jeans and brushed her bangs out of her eyes with the back of her hand. Whoever stood by the buzzer had more determination than she did. "Who is it?" she called out.

"Mike."

Her stomach flipped, but she grabbed for the doorknob before she could change her mind. "We've got to stop meeting like this."

"And we would if you'd answer your cell." He grinned. "May I?" He gestured inside and, without waiting for an answer, slid past her into the apartment.

"Pushy," she muttered.

"So I've been told," he called over his shoulder.

"You weren't supposed to hear that." Despite her late-night resolution to steer clear of Peter's brother, she couldn't deny she was glad to see him. She shut the door, turned and followed him inside.

"To what do I owe the pleasure?" she asked.

He stood by the window overlooking the small park. Wearing ragged denim shorts and a black T-shirt, his impact was as potent as ever.

"I thought we should talk." He crossed his muscular forearms over his chest.

Idly she wondered if he worked out and where. She'd love to watch him develop those biceps. She licked her suddenly dry lips. The Carly Wexler she knew never had such wayward thoughts about men.

He pushed himself off the wall and took two steps toward her. The sexy swagger and casual air, that were so much a part of him, never ceased to amaze her. Neither did the fact that he was related to Peter. And that was the thought that sobered her.

"Talk about what?" she asked warily.

"What happened last night."

She folded her arms across her chest. "Nothing happened."

His eyes narrowed, pinning her in place. "Funny, but you didn't strike me as a coward."

She ignored that comment. "We were on a crowded dance floor. Nothing happened." *If you don't acknowledge it, it can't hurt you.* Her mother's voice echoed inside her head. Tears she'd suppressed late in the night rushed forth, threatening to fall at the slightest provocation.

"Why did I know you'd say that?"

She swiped at her bangs, then tucked a stray strand of hair behind her ear. "Because it's true."

He held up his hands in a mock gesture of surrender. "You win. For now," he muttered. "It's a beautiful day. Too nice to spend inside." He glanced around, taking in the rags, cleaning solutions and Good Will boxes scattered around the room. "Definitely too nice to spend indoors cleaning."

"Got any better ideas?" Carly regretted the words the minute they left her mouth.

A knowing smirk formed on his lips. "I do. Do you like amusement parks?"

"Who doesn't?" Peter. The traitorous thought formed and she pushed it aside. If he'd returned her call before going to the office, maybe he'd be here now instead of Mike. Then again, knowing Peter, maybe not. Work came first, after all.

She forced a smile. "Disliking amusement parks and carnivals is un-American."

"So I don't have to pour on the charm to convince you." He grinned. "Well? What are you waiting for?" He prodded her gently on the back. "Go get changed, unless you don't mind roasting in those heavy jeans."

"You're serious." How could she go anywhere with him and keep a clear conscience?

"Of course. I rented a car. Playland is a short half-hour ride from here, or haven't you heard?"

The last good memory she had of her father was a Sunday when he'd taken her to Playland. "Have you been there before?" she asked, stalling for time.

"Grew up near there."

"That's right, I forgot."

"You're stalling," he said with dead-on accuracy. "Are you coming or not?" he asked.

Playland. She reached back into pleasant childhood memories and felt the beginning of a relaxed smile take hold, her first in a long while. Mike reached his bronzed hand toward her. She hesitated, and silence stretched taut between them.

Carly listened to the conflicting voices deep inside her before making a decision. Finally, she placed her hand inside his. Just this once she'd follow her heart.

*　　*　　*

Carly looked down at her hand firmly enclosed in Mike's strong grasp. Crazy Glue couldn't bond more thoroughly than she and Mike had over the past few hours. Unable to resist the opportunity to spend time with him, she had broken her self-imposed promise to keep her distance. One time wouldn't hurt, she'd rationalized. She now wondered how much rationalizing her father had done during his affair with his twenty-five-year-old secretary.

She gazed around the park and listened to the shouts coming from the brazen riders of the Dragon Coaster, the Tilt-a-Whirl and the Spider. With the exception of the carousel, she had laid her head on Mike's chest and screamed through each ride. She had loved every heart-stopping minute spent in his arms.

Juggling her newly won stuffed animals, she gingerly tugged on Mike's sleeve. When he turned, she gestured toward the cotton candy concession stand.

"Two snow cones, one hot dog and a bag of popcorn weren't enough for you?" he asked with a grin.

She shrugged.

He pulled his wallet from his pants pocket. "I'll say one thing, you're not a cheap date."

"Maybe not, but I'm a fun one." She laughed. "And I'm not the one who wasted almost fifty dollars trying to win that oversized bear."

"No, but who was it who sighed and said 'Oh, he'd look so cute sitting in my living room'?"

"Guilty." She grinned. "And it was kind of you to accommodate me." She thought of the cuddly pink bear that now rested comfortably on the backseat of the rental car. "How's the pitching arm?" She gave his muscled biceps a playful squeeze, drawing her hand back before she succumbed to temptation and explored further.

He grunted and handed her the cloud of spun sugar.

"I love cotton candy." Taking a bite of the pink fluff, she closed her eyes and let the sugar dissolve in her mouth. "Heaven."

"Show me."

At the sound of his deep voice, her eyes popped open wide.

"Just a little taste." The laugh lines crinkled around his eyes. "Please."

Before she could change her mind, she stuck one finger into the ball of pink fluff. "Open." She barely recognized her own voice.

Mike complied. She raised her sugar-laden finger and placed it into his waiting mouth, watching intently as his lips closed around her finger. Warm, wet and welcoming. A rush of dizziness assaulted her, but that was like a small wave compared to the heady rush she received when he nibbled on her fingertip with his teeth. A tidal wave of sensations surged through her. Such a simple act threatened her very being.

She wanted what she'd never realized she was capable of wanting. What she'd never *allowed* herself to desire. She wanted passion. Wanted to soothe the ache that pounded in every part of her body. She wanted Mike.

And she couldn't allow it.

Slowly, she pulled back, wiping her now cool finger against her denim shorts. "Well," she murmured. Flustered and embarrassed, she turned away.

Mike cleared his throat. "You and Pete do this often?" he asked.

"What?" His question had her pivoting back to face him in an instant.

He smiled, the charming grin that came naturally but knocked the wind right out of her.

"Carnivals. Do you and Pete do this sort of thing often?" he asked.

"Oh." She exhaled a sigh of relief. "No." They talked, ate in fancy restaurants when he wasn't working, attended work-related functions. His and hers, but mostly his. Not once did they let loose and have fun.

Why had she allowed herself to believe that was enough for her? Because safety and security were more important to her than a good time. Had her feelings changed so drastically in such a short period of time, or was Mike just the catalyst, forcing her to face things she'd buried for too long?

"I guess Peter doesn't relax often enough to enjoy something like this," Mike said.

"No, he doesn't."

"It's a shame. He used to love this place when we were kids."

"Did your parents take you?" She immediately placed a hand on his arm. "I'm sorry," she murmured. "That was thoughtless. I was comparing my own childhood to yours and spoke without thinking." How could she have been so careless?

He shrugged. "No problem. Pete and I were abandoned a long time ago. We made out okay."

His words startled her. He smiled, but she didn't buy the act. Orphaned wasn't the same as abandoned. She wondered if he recognized the distinction.

"What happened?" she asked.

"Pete never told you?"

She shook her head. "Not in detail." And she hadn't pushed. So why force Mike to talk now?

He exhaled a sigh. "My aunt and uncle weren't the best parents. Very little love and even less laughter." He spoke without rancor, but as he looked over the park, he clenched his jaw and donned a closed expression. The carefree man of earlier in the afternoon had disappeared.

Obviously he hadn't come to terms with his past as completely as he'd have her believe. That was something she could relate to. "So that's why you two are so close, even when you're not on the same continent," she said.

"Yeah. We didn't choose the same paths, but we're close."

"Looks like the Novack brothers made good."

He shrugged. "One brother never stays in one place and the other looks for the easy way. I'm not sure I'd call that making good."

"Law school isn't taking the easy way," she reminded him. Neither was traveling the globe to the world's hot spots.

"No, but in Pete's mind, success in law school guaranteed money. Another thing in short supply growing up."

The sudden insight into her fiancé astounded her... not just because she had thought she understood Peter and didn't, but because her information came from Mike and not the man she was about to marry.

Mike glanced at her, a serious expression clouding his handsome features. "Pete's willing to sacrifice an awful lot to achieve his goals."

She pondered his words. "Life's full of sacrifices."

"Do you want to be one of them?" He waved away his words with a jerk of his hand. "What I meant was, sacrifice is fine as long as you don't give up what counts."

What counts for you, Mike? Though she wanted to

know, she was more afraid of hearing his response.

So the question remained unasked—and unanswered.

"Hey. You up for one last ride before we go home?" He pointed toward the large Ferris wheel and all other thoughts fled.

"You bet." She turned and ran toward the ride. The fact that she was also running from her thoughts didn't escape her notice.

*   *   *

Mike followed a short distance behind Carly, admiring the sexy sway of her hips as she sprinted ahead. Until today, when he'd seen her in those brief cutoff shorts, he hadn't realized how long her legs actually were. Long enough for a good many things, he realized, halting his thoughts before he embarrassed himself in a public place.

She stopped at the entrance to the ride and swung around. "Hey, are you coming or am I riding this thing alone?"

He grinned and caught up with her. All afternoon her enthusiasm had been contagious, making him glad he'd stopped by Pete's apartment to retrieve his camera. Though he'd been unwilling to look at the damn thing up until now, an afternoon in the sunshine with Carly provided a not-to-be missed opportunity.

He'd enjoyed today more than any other in recent memory. And he knew... the shots he'd taken today would have to last him a lifetime.

The day had been full of revelations, though. If he'd had an inkling before, he now realized how mismatched Carly and his brother actually were. Although he had no right to judge, no right to come between them, the idea of letting them end up together, making each other miserable, ate at his gut. So did the never-ending sense of guilt. Technically he'd done nothing wrong, yet he couldn't shake the nagging feeling that he was betraying his brother.

Stepping back, he allowed her to precede him onto the ride. He handed the operator the tickets and a tip, pointing to the top of the Ferris wheel. The teenager, obviously used to such requests, slapped Mike on the back and winked.

After taking his place next to Carly, Mike nudged her in the ribs. "Drop the loot. We'll scoop up the animals when the ride's over."

"Do I have to?" She looked like a child ordered to retire her favorite toy.

He nodded. "If I can drop the camera, you can drop the winnings."

"I get attached quickly," she said, obviously embarrassed. But she scattered them around the small area at their feet.

He wished she'd get attached to him that fast and immediately banished the thought.

"So what are your plans?" Carly asked on their third trip around.

"I got a temporary job working for a city paper."

"How temporary?"

He wondered that himself. A light breeze surrounded them, causing tendrils of hair to caress her face. The sounds of the park and the realities of life seemed far away. When the huge wheel stranded them at the summit, Carly hung her head over the side in an attempt to discern the problem.

With a gentle tug, he pulled her back into the car. "Relax, it'll get started again soon."

She sat back in her seat and spoke so quietly he had to strain to hear. "You didn't answer me. How long before you're off and running to the next trouble spot in the world?" she asked, looking off into the clear blue sky.

"No specific date." And right now, leaving was the furthest thing from his mind. With Carly sitting beside him, nothing else seemed to matter. Not a good sign, he thought. "But when the call comes, I'll be ready."

He cleared his throat. "Why didn't you tell Pete about the book?" he asked, changing the subject.

She remained silent, refusing to acknowledge his question.

"What about the rings?"

"What about them?" she asked.

"You loved those other rings."

She didn't refute his statement and Mike wondered. If he kept pushing, would she realize that she and his brother were mismatched opposites? Would she call things off before two people got hurt? Did he want her to?

Hell, he didn't need that responsibility. He could walk her through this now, but he wouldn't be there for her in the long run. His lifestyle wasn't suited to the white picket fence and security she so obviously sought.

If he pushed, he could end up hurting her as badly as his brother could. Helluva pair he and Pete made. He shook his head. "You really love him, don't you?" Mike asked.

"Who?"

He stared. "Peter. Who else?" He held his breath waiting for her answer. An answer that shouldn't matter to him, but dammit, it did.

"Oh. Yes. Of course." She answered without meeting his gaze, a sure indication that his gut instincts were on target.

Since those same instincts had saved his behind many times, he hadn't really been in doubt.

She turned her attention from the cloudless sky,

fingering her bangs with trembling hands.

"You do that a lot."

"What?" she asked.

"This." With a slow but steady hand, he ran his fingers through her bangs. She swallowed, and his eyes were drawn to the slender column of her neck. In silence, she glanced up at him from beneath thick lashes before lowering her eyes. He had no doubt she hoped to hide the feelings he'd seen reflected there. She'd been unsuccessful.

He tried to speak but words wouldn't come. Instead, as the silky strands of hair grazed his hands, he ached with the intensity of his feelings for this woman he'd known such a short time.

He trailed one finger down the side of her face until his hand rested beneath her chin. He tilted her head upward. Acting on impulse and not common sense, he lowered his head until his lips brushed hers. Whisper soft and brief, but that light touch stirred his body to life.

She sucked in a deep breath but didn't attempt to break the tenuous connection between them. Mike did, drawing himself back with extreme difficulty.

Looking at her flushed face and full lips, he knew, without a doubt, she had never felt this way about his brother. Not in the past, not now and especially not in the future. He was certain, not because of conceit or arrogance, but because he'd never experienced anything like the magic of being with Carly. Something that powerful could not be one-sided.

He pushed aside the guilt that continued to plague him at the thought of Peter. His brother didn't care about this woman, not the way an engaged man ought to care about his fiancé.

And Mike couldn't offer her much better. But that didn't mean he could remain silent much longer. He cared about her too much to watch her throw her life away. "We need to talk," he said.

Her lower lip trembled and she shook her head.

"It can't wait, Carly. You've been so busy planning that you haven't dealt with… things. I don't want to see you or Peter hurt."

She turned wet, shadowed eyes toward him. "I would never hurt your brother."

At that moment the mechanism on the Ferris wheel kicked into gear and they began their descent. "Damn," he muttered. "That wasn't what I meant. You and I…"

"Forget it." Eyes wide, she spoke with something akin to fear in her voice.

"No. We're getting off this ride and sitting down someplace to talk."

She backed into the corner of the small car. "No. We're getting off this ride, collecting my animals and going home. We'll listen to the radio and talk about comfortable things but nothing remotely personal." Without looking in his direction, she scrambled to gather her prizes.

They reached the bottom. The ride's operator waited for Mike to exit before extending his hand and helping Carly from the car. He patted Mike on the back. "Enough time for you and your lady to enjoy?" he asked with a chuckle.

"Not nearly," he muttered. He had to sprint to keep up with Carly, who appeared to be running for her life.

*   *   *

Mike reached out and turned off the car radio. Carly felt his steady gaze. She clenched her jaw and flipped the stereo back on. Easy-listening music filled her ears but wasn't nearly loud or distracting enough. She fiddled with the dial until she found hard rock. His hand reached out and stilled her frantic movements.

"What's bothering you?" he asked.

"Nothing. We had a great time."

"Am I wrong in thinking there's a connection between us?"

She didn't want to hear this. She had kissed him while engaged to another man. Kissed him while engaged to his brother, she amended. Worse, she had enjoyed it. Apparently her father's blood flowed through her veins after all. "Don't you love carnivals?" she asked, changing the subject.

"Carly, do you trust me?"

"Of course. That's a stupid question. How did you fit that bear in the backseat anyway?" She fidgeted uncomfortably, hoping he would take her not-too-subtle hint and drop the idea of discussing *them*.

"I stuffed it in headfirst." He muttered a curse and slammed his hand against the steering wheel.

Ignoring his agitation, she turned the radio louder. She replayed their first meeting and today's brief kiss in her mind. Her traitorous body responded to the mere thought of his lips on hers. Two men at the same time. Two brothers, no less. And she thought her father should be tarred and feathered? With a groan she laid her head against the car window.

He made a few more attempts to draw her into any kind of conversation, which she childishly ignored, pretending instead to be asleep. Finally he lapsed into blessed silence. She knew her behavior was infantile, but she couldn't help feeling relieved nevertheless.

Anything he might have said would only reinforce the fact that each time she let her guard down around Mike, she lost a little more self-control.

She and Mike were an explosion waiting to happen and Carly knew one thing for certain. Explosions, once they occurred, were impossible to control.

*   *   *

This afternoon, Mike had visited heaven. Now he prepared himself for hell. Sure, Pete had asked him to watch out for Carly and help with last-minute wedding details. But he hadn't asked Mike to take his fiancé out for the day, nor had he asked him to kiss her... or enjoy the experience quite so much. Pete also hadn't asked Mike to push her into questioning her upcoming marriage.

Mike muttered a curse. He approached Pete's apartment with as much excitement as a man facing a firing squad. Turning the key in the lock, he silently prayed for the strength to do the right thing for everyone involved. Damned if he knew what that was.

He stepped into the dimly lit apartment. "Hey, Pete, you back yet?" Silence greeted him, granting him a temporary reprieve. He tossed the keys on a shelf near the door and walked inside unprepared for what he saw.

Pete and a young woman sat on the floor of the living room poring over files and legal briefs. They didn't glance up, obviously too engrossed in work to have heard him come in. Nothing unusual or unto-ward about that, Mike thought.

Unless you knew Peter. The last time Mike had

seen Pete casually dressed, they'd been teenagers... and he'd asked Mike for pointers on how to dress to impress the opposite sex. Looking at his brother now, Mike suppressed a groan.

Dressed in one of Mike's Polo shirts, a pair of khaki chinos and Docksiders, his brother looked like he'd stepped out of a Ralph Lauren ad. The woman gave the appearance of a little pixie, but based on Carly's description, he'd guess barracuda would be more accurate.

Mike walked into the room and was about to say hello when Pete burst out laughing, prompting the attractive associate to place a manicured hand on his shoulder and laugh with him. Her bare feet nudged Peter's calf. Then, as if a silent understanding had been reached, they returned to their respective files and work.

Innocent, and yet... Mike shook his head. He ought to throttle his brother, but even as the thought took hold, he felt the vise that had gripped his heart for the last few weeks lessen and ease, until breathing became effortless.

"Hi." Mike cleared his throat. "Sorry to interrupt."

His brother glanced up from his seat on the floor. "No big deal. We were just finishing up some work." Pete stood, then reached out a hand to help the woman up from the floor.

Was it Mike's imagination or did her fingers linger seconds too long before releasing Peter's hand?

"Regina Grey, this is my brother, Mike." Pete smiled. "Mike, Regina."

Mike shook the dainty hand she held out toward him. "Nice to meet you."

"Same here." Regina began collecting items off the floor. "I just want to go over some things at home and we can meet first thing Monday morning and discuss strategy," she said.

"I'll be there."

No haggling, no bargaining, no compromise. Interesting, Mike thought.

When Peter returned from escorting the pretty Miss Grey to her cab, Mike turned on his brother. "What the hell's with you?" Mike asked.

Pete bent to retrieve the documents Regina had left behind. "What? The air-conditioning broke in the office and we came back here to work."

Mike waved a dismissive hand in the air. "I don't mean that." But he didn't know how to approach the subject with his brother. He raked a hand through his hair. "What is it with you two?"

"Who?" Pete asked, his brows crinkling in confusion.

"You and Carly, that's who." After shoving his hands in the front pockets of his shorts, Mike began pacing the room. "You laugh with this Regina?" he asked finally.

"She's quick."

"And bright. And pretty…"

"So is Carly," Pete chimed in. Too late, Mike thought.

"And an attorney," Mike continued as if he hadn't heard his brother speak. "And you have a hell of a lot more in common with her than you do with your fiancé, if you don't mind my saying so."

"You've always spoken your mind before," Pete said. "But this is my life, Mike. We didn't have parents to meddle in our lives as kids. I sure as hell don't need you to do it now."

"You're going through with this marriage, then?"

"The end result was never in question." Pete groaned and sat down on the leather sofa. "What she doesn't know won't hurt her."

"You're dead wrong. You may not mean to, but you'll destroy Carly and suffocate yourself." Forget what this marriage would do to him, Mike thought "Is that a way to live?"

His brother didn't answer.

"Pete, you're not…" Mike trailed off. As close as the brothers had always been, they'd never traded sexual exploits, and Mike had no desire to start now. Still, he couldn't protect Carly if he didn't know the truth.

And though no one had appointed him her keeper, he'd taken on the role as if it was meant for him alone. "You're not sleeping with Regina, are you?"

Pete stared from his seat on the couch. His silence pronounced him guilty.

Mike let out a groan. "For the love of…"

Pete had the grace to look ashamed. "I thought I could wait, but…"

Sweet and innocent. How the hell had she gotten involved with either one of the Novack brothers? Each had the power to break her heart.

Pete shrugged. "We've been engaged for the last five months and dated on and off for three before that. A guy certainly can't go that long without…"

"He damn well can," Mike shouted. "And if you loved her, you would have."

"If she loved me, I wouldn't have had to look somewhere else," Pete retorted.

Mike clenched his teeth. "And what does that tell you?"

"Go back to globe-trotting and let me handle my own life." Apparently, Pete was about to dig in his heels as hard as Carly had. Neither wanted to face reality.

Considering Mike had abandoned his own reality, he had no right to force theirs on them. "Just don't be surprised when things backfire."

Peter glared at him through narrowed, suspicious eyes. "Mind your own business," he said, clearly warning Mike to keep his mouth shut.

"Because you think your partnership's at stake?"

"Possibly."

"Then why'd you bring Regina back here? You know I'm staying over. Or did you take that risk on purpose?"

He couldn't stomach being in this apartment for another minute. Mike turned, scooped his keys off the counter and grabbed his camera from the front hall closet.

"Don't tell her, Mike." Pete's words reverberated in his head as he walked out, slamming the door behind him.

*   *   *

Parents and children, men and their dates, guys and their dogs and one lone man with his camera romped in Central Park. Mike wandered around, snapping photos without paying much attention to the setup. Each shot captured life in a way he treasured. Each would have a spot in his private collection. A select few he'd bring downtown to his new editor. He wasn't used to soft pieces, but after the hard stories he'd covered until recently, he welcomed the reprieve.

Until today, he'd retired his camera to the depths of Peter's closet, hoping to banish the unpleasant memories that went with it. To his surprise, when he'd picked up the camera and snapped the first shot, the rush of adrenaline had been powerful and positive. Of course, it had helped that Carly was his first subject.

If only he could view his life the same upbeat way. During his last assignment, he'd hitched a ride home from the countryside. Close to civilization, mortar fire hit the back tires of a bus ahead of him, sending it careening down the side of a ravine. Nothing Mike hadn't seen hundreds of times before in cities with different names. By the time he'd reached the bus, the smell of gasoline permeated the air. He and his companion managed to get the survivors out before the explosion hit. Jagged metal ripped through the muscle in his right shoulder. Just the memory made him break into a sweat and he wiped the back of his hand over his brow.

All those young kids abandoned because their mothers had sat in the front of the bus while they played in the back. The luck of the draw, something Mike had also seen too many times before. All the carnival food he'd eaten with Carly threatened to come back up.

Over the next few weeks, he was sidelined with his injury. He'd used the time to help track down the kids' fathers or other living relatives. Most had already been killed. All those children, orphaned like Mike and Peter. And though his boss had ordered him back to the center of the conflict once the doctors gave him a clean bill of health, Mike had bailed out instead.

He'd left mid-assignment, hopping the first plane back to the States. Three weeks early for his brother's wedding... or just in time, depending on one's place in this awful triangle, he thought wryly.

He glanced down at the camera in his hand, a piece of equipment that felt as comfortable as his own skin. At that moment, Mike knew. No matter what memories or doubts haunted him, he'd be facing them sooner rather than later. When his boss called—and he would—Mike wouldn't hesitate. Though Dom had finally given in on the extended leave issue, he swore that the next hot story was Mike's. Mike trusted his boss and friend not only to give him the time he needed, but to drag his butt back out there as soon as he could afterward. It would be the push he needed to return.

He'd be going back to the only life he knew. Carly's face flashed in front of his eyes. But in facing his past, he'd be leaving her behind... and exchanging one set of painful memories for another.

FIVE

F ive days and no word from Mike. With her wedding a little over a week away, Carly knew she ought to feel relieved. Life went on, and Peter had even managed to get out of work early one night and take her for dinner. A sure sign things were looking up. If one believed in signs. These days, Carly took any good omen she could get.

She put the finishing touches on her last column before summer repeats began and hit the print button. She'd drop the printout at Juliette's later in the week. Glancing at her watch, she realized she couldn't put off the inevitable any longer and headed uptown for her fitting. Since she hadn't been in touch with Mike, she hoped she could safely assume she was on her own.

She entered the bridal showroom where she'd purchased her gown, grateful the place wasn't crowded. With a little luck, this would be over in no time. Minutes later, the salesgirl, who had taken her name, reappeared with a long garment bag draped over her arm. One glance at the zippered bag and Carly's stomach did a nervous flip. Before the salesgirl could lead Carly back to the fitting room, she was paged to the front of the store.

She smiled, apologetically, and hung the gown from a hook on the side wall. "I'll be right back."

"I'll be here." Alone, Carly stared at the white bag, her stomach fluttering nonstop. Inside was the dress she'd wear when she married Peter. When she became Mrs. Peter Novack. When her life would be changed forever.

She pushed aside the nagging knowledge that something was terribly wrong. Since the fateful day she'd met Mike on the street, a tiny seed of doubt had taken root. She'd denied it, starved it, but it wouldn't go away. Now wasn't the time to examine it too closely. Once Mike was gone, life would return to normal. Safe, calm and peaceful.

She fingered the engagement ring, thinking of the wedding bands they'd chosen. Make that the bands *Peter* had chosen. She'd explained her feelings, but Peter had held firm. Despite her protests and explanations that stopped short of outright pleading, he'd been adamant. Had she broken down and cried, Peter would have succumbed in an instant, but she refused to resort to feminine manipulation to get her way. Obviously, Peter's reasons meant more to him than she'd realized. For the sake of peace and Peter's happiness, she'd compromised. Again.

The one thing about this wedding that hadn't been a compromise lay in that bag.

"Go ahead and take a peek."

Carly whirled around to face Mike. "You startled me." She placed a hand over her chest in a futile effort to calm her rapidly beating heart. "What are you doing here?"

"We had a date." Mike lifted one eyebrow, as if daring her to dispute his statement.

"I didn't think you'd show up."

"I try to honor my commitments," he said with complete sincerity.

She chose to ignore that comment. "How'd you find me?"

He leaned against the wall and grinned. His smile had the ability to stop her heart each and every time. She ground her teeth hard. "Well?"

"One phone call and a very efficient secretary. Did you ever think of giving her a raise?"

"Don't look so smug."

"And don't you look so unhappy. You know you're glad to see me."

She couldn't hide her smile. "Your ego astounds me."

"Can I have a look?" he asked, walking over to the

garment bag. He reached for the zipper.

She smacked his hand. "Let me." With Mike staring from behind, she felt shy about looking at the dress she'd be wearing to wed another man. She bit her lower lip and gingerly unzipped the bag.

Reaching inside, she withdrew the material, gaping at the gown in shock. "It's pink!"

Mike stepped back to appraise the dress and let out a long, approving whistle. "Nice," he murmured his gaze taking in the scooped neckline and intricate beading.

"It's pink." Her hand gripped his arm and her fingernails dug into his skin.

"I admit it's a surprise." And not just for him, Mike thought, judging by the horrified look on Carly's face. "You ordered white." Not a difficult guess.

After his brother's slip a few days before, Mike realized Carly was truly innocent. Not that most brides didn't wear white regardless, but Carly had maintained the right. Forget what Peter's reaction would be to his bride walking down the aisle in anything but traditional white, she deserved to have her first choice. After all her compromising, she shouldn't have to give in on something as important as her wedding gown.

He turned toward her, startled to see tears running down her face. "Hey," he said, brushing at the drop of moisture with his thumb. "I'm sure this can be fixed."

He hoped.

"It's an omen."

"Come on, you don't believe in that stuff." He, on the other hand, agreed wholeheartedly.

"I planned this wedding and nothing has gone as I wanted... No one has given a single thought to my feelings, but this..." She lifted the lace edge of the gown. "This was mine." She groaned. "Or it was supposed to be."

"Carly," he began carefully, "think about what you just said."

"So much for the perfect wedding."

She wasn't listening. He grabbed her by both arms, as if he were grabbing his last chance to reach her. "The *perfect* wedding won't change the fact that both people involved are far from the *perfect* couple. All the planning in the world won't change that."

The look of pain on her face almost destroyed him.

"How dare you?"

He swore silently. "I dare because you don't. Listen to yourself. Nothing about this wedding has turned out the way you wanted it. No one, including my brother, who I love but who can also be an ass, has given a damn about your needs."

She tried to jerk her arms free, but he held on fast. "What does that tell you?" he asked.

"That this is none of your business." She wrenched free from his grasp.

"You're right, but I can't sit around and watch this farce any longer. If I don't point out what you can't face, what kind of friend am I?" He shoved his fingers through his hair. *What kind of brother am I?*

She cocked her head to one side. Though her eyes remained wet and her pain was almost tangible, he sensed she was listening. At last.

"Look, sweetheart, you're two different people with two different personalities. It doesn't make either of you wrong or a bad person. That's just the way it is and it's time you faced the truth."

"What gives you the right to pass judgment?" she asked.

"Not a damn thing. But I love my brother and I… care about you. Marriage is forever. Promise me you'll think about that."

"And do what? Break off my engagement a week before the wedding?" Her voice cracked under the strain.

"If that's what feels right, then yes."

"I made a *commitment*." She paced the small area before turning on him. "Do you even know what the word means?"

"Carly…" he said, warning her with his tone. "Don't make this personal."

"And what is it but personal? How can someone like you give me advice? What do you know about the long haul? About sticking with someone, for better or for worse?" She paused for air. "When things get tough, there's always that first flight out, isn't there?"

"I'll ignore the insult. We're discussing you, remember? For better or worse doesn't apply yet, sweetheart. And I suggest you get the hell out before it does." He exhaled, unable to believe he'd said the words that were on his tongue since day one.

Her eyes narrowed. "You have no right."

"Maybe not, but if you marry my brother, you're running the same way you think I am. I haven't figured out why yet but I recognize the signs. Only difference between you and me is, when you wake up one morning with your heart and soul in pieces, you and your so-called commitment are stuck for good."

He glanced at Carly, expecting her to come at him swinging. Instead, she sat in a chair and wrapped her arms around herself like a lost child. The sight pierced his heart. Though he wanted to hold her, she probably wouldn't let him near.

Just as well, he told himself. Now that he'd had his say, the rest was up to her. "You've got some decisions to make before it's too late." He drew a deep breath. "You say you're tired of compromise? Prove it."

She raised her head from where her chin rested on

her knees. Her eyes mirrored her soul. Pain, anger, hurt, anguish… and a myriad of other emotions Mike couldn't decipher melded in the dark depths.

"Do me a favor?" she asked in a soft voice.

"Anything." He took two steps toward her.

"Get the hell out and leave me alone."

*   *   *

Juliette slid into the seat across from Carly at a small restaurant on Madison Avenue. "You could have faxed your column in or dropped it off at the office." She glanced back at the cases of baked goods, muffins, breads and scones. "But I'd much rather meet for food. I'm starving."

She shook the green linen napkin out in front of her and placed it on her lap. "Orange pekoe tea, please," she said to a passing waitress.

The younger woman paused. "Anything for you?" she asked, turning to Carly.

"Coffee."

"Chamomile tea," Juliette said. She leaned closer to Carly. "Your hands are shaking. The last thing you need is caffeine."

Carly glanced at the waitress and shrugged.

"Chamomile's fine." She wasn't here for food, just motherly advice and maybe a hug.

The waitress replaced her pad and walked away.

Juliette narrowed her eyes. "What's going on? You gave in too easily."

"Why is it everyone thinks I'm a lapdog? I make my own decisions. I even put on a different shade of eyeshadow this morning," Carly said, defiance in her voice.

"I said you're *too* compliant, meaning I've never known you to back down from an argument with me in your life."

Carly sighed. "That's professional."

"And you're damn good at what you do. So while I was making an observation that something's wrong because you're not behaving like your confident self, *someone else* obviously sees you differently." Juliette leaned back for the waitress to set down their cups, choice of tea and hot water. "Who?"

Carly needed to unburden herself with a desperation she'd never known before. And she trusted Juliette to listen without passing judgment and to offer the comfort she needed. "His name is Mike," she said softly. "Mike Novack."

"Peter's…"

"Brother," Carly finished for her.

"Good Lord, when you dive in, you really do it with both feet."

"You don't know the half of it." She drew a deep breath. "Jules… I don't think I can marry Peter," Carly said in a whisper. Then, to keep busy, she unwrapped the tea bag with shaking hands and let it steep in the steaming water.

Her friend braced her chin in her hands. "Go on. I don't want to influence you one way or another until I hear what's going through your mind. Keep talking."

"It's hard to explain. It's like, up until now, I've gone through life in a fog and now the mist has cleared. I *feel*."

Juliette nodded. "And it scares the living daylights out of you."

"That's putting it mildly." What Mike did for her, to her and with her, reminded her of everything she'd sworn off early in life. Her father had destroyed her illusions, her perfect family, and worse, another human being. If that was the result of so-called love and passion, Carly could live without it.

But she couldn't compromise herself to be Peter's perfect mate. Not anymore. In fact, she couldn't believe she'd convinced herself it was for the best. She'd observed her mother doing that kind of compliance, and for years, Carly had silently condemned her for it. Yet in an effort to break free of her father's actions, she'd somehow believed she would be happy with that kind of bland life.

Thanks to Mike's appearance, she now knew better. In that respect, his observations had been on target. "Mike scares me," she admitted. "But he isn't what this is about."

Juliette raised an eyebrow, looking skeptical. "Okay, then. Peter's brother arrives from…"

"Overseas."

"Overseas. Knocks you off your feet, makes you reconsider marrying Peter, thank the good Lord, but *he* isn't what this life-altering decision is about?"

"No." The excuse sounded lame to Carly, too. But no matter how much Mike Novack affected her, he was not a part of her future. "The man is sexy and sweet, but he's just passing through my life."

"What if he's not? Every person has that perfect mate out there, Carly. What if he's the one?"

She closed her eyes, wishing it was possible. But instead of happily ever after, all she saw were the pictures Mike had graphically described to her. War zones and traveling, danger and excitement. Those things appealed to Mike. He wasn't the kind of man who wanted a wife and kids back home, or people to answer to.

And she wasn't the kind of woman who would accept any less. Once he was gone, he was out of her life forever. They both knew it. "Even if he's the one, Jules, he's just not the staying kind of guy."

* * *

Now that the decision had been made, Carly needed to get it over with as soon as possible. She drew a deep breath and with a trembling hand let herself into Peter's office.

"Hi." For his sake, she forced a smile.

"Hello." He stood, then adjusted his tie. His gaze traveled over her, his brows crinkling with concern. "You look exhausted."

"I am. Can I sit?" she asked, avoiding the urge to wring her hands. She had too much nervous energy building up inside her. She wasn't sure she could get through telling him. Nor was she sure *how* to tell him without hurting him, something she did not want to do.

"Sure." He gestured to the chair across from his desk. Carly sat, feeling more like a client than his fiancé. The signs had been there all along. She had just chosen not to heed them.

"I've got just a few minutes before the department meeting, so…"

She clenched her jaw, which only added to the building headache she'd had for the past few days. Even before talking to Juliette, she'd agonized over Mike's blunt words in the bridal shop. Hearing her own fears verbalized by someone else, especially Mike, had sent her into a panic. Fight or flight, she now realized. She'd chosen first to fight Mike and then to run from the truth in his words. After two days locked in a battle with herself, she could now face the truth.

She fingered the strap on her purse and wondered how in the world to begin. "I know you hate unexpected surprises, but this is important." And that was but one problem. Each time Peter ignored her for work or squeezed her in as an inconvenience to be tolerated, he put a serious dent in not only their relationship but in her self-esteem.

She deserved better.

"Like I said, I've got a few minutes. What's wrong?" he asked.

"What isn't wrong?" She leaned forward. "I don't know how to say this except to just... say it. I want... I need... that is, I don't think this marriage will work." She forced the words out, then exhaled in relief.

She dared a glance at Peter's face. Shock and disbelief crossed his features. "You what?"

She swallowed over the lump in her throat. "We're different. It's so obvious you can't miss it... unless, of course, you want to." Or aren't paying attention, she thought sadly. "Take the wedding: I compromised on every major issue. The caterers, the color scheme, the rings..."

"If this is about those plain rings, we'll cancel the original order and go back to buy those."

Too little, too late, she thought.

"You should have said something sooner."

"I did. Over and over." Not that it had made a difference in their relationship. Wedding arrangements should have solidified the bond between them, not driven them farther apart. Their relationship had disintegrated and neither one had acknowledged the warning signs in time to rectify the problem. If Peter searched his heart as she had searched her own, would he also discover that he really hadn't cared enough to bother? They'd each wanted something out of their relationship. Unfortunately they'd been two people with parallel goals. Their needs and desires had never crossed.

She glanced up at him through watery eyes. "You never wanted to hear."

"All couples go through last-minute jitters right before the wedding. I'm sure we can work things out. Compromise on some issues, things like that."

Laughter bubbled from within, threatening to erupt in tears or hysterics, she wasn't sure which. She shook her head. "No more, Peter." She'd made her decision and intended to stick with it. The determination in her voice took her by surprise.

Peter slammed his hand on the desk. "I knew I couldn't trust my do-gooder brother." Peter stood and walked around the desk, kneeling in front of her. "If this is about Regina, it's over. I swear she has nothing to do with us. She never did. From now on…"

Carly tried to absorb Peter's words and meaning, but her head whirled and she couldn't manage to think straight. Feelings, however, pulsed through her, their message clear. Betrayal, pain and anger. Every reason she'd picked Peter as her *safe* fiancé disintegrated in front of her eyes.

And as his excuses turned to pleading, she rose from her chair, obviously too fast because the room began to spin around her and she leaned against the wall for support. Somehow, she couldn't bring herself to believe the truth. "Are you telling me you cheated on me?" Carly needed to hear the words.

"You didn't know?"

"No." *But Mike did.* And that, Carly realized, hurt most of all.

She swallowed hard. "Well, I'm only sorry I lost so much sleep agonizing over how to tell you." She wrapped the remains of her tattered pride around her like a warm cloak, but nothing helped ease the chill inside her heart.

"Carly, please." He rose and stood beside her.

"Please what?" she asked. "Don't do this?" She shook her head. "It took everything inside me to do what's right for both us, while you never once thought of me."

"That's not true." He placed his hand on her arm.

She shook off his grasp. "Don't touch me."

"I'm sorry."

A brief knock jolted Carly into sudden awareness of her surroundings. She might not agree with how her mother had lived her life, but one lesson Carly had learned well: Keep private things private and never wear your heart on your sleeve. Although she'd never agreed with her mother's refusal to discuss the pain that rocked their lives, Carly suddenly understood that defense mechanism better than ever before. A lawyer's office was no place for theatrics or confrontations, and her emotions were hers. Peter didn't deserve to know how badly his betrayal had hurt her.

The door behind her swung open wide. Mike stood in the door frame. In his standard denim jeans, black T-shirt and hiking boots, he looked sexy and masculine. A man confident in his own skin.

She shook her head. Her conservative ex-fiancé had never stood a chance. With a flash of insight, she realized that Mike appealed to her wilder side. The part she'd tried, unsuccessfully, to suffocate. To hide.

Seeking comfort from Peter's admission, and what she viewed as Mike's betrayal as well as her own, she wrapped her arms around her chest. "What a great time for a family reunion," she muttered.

"Okay, what the hell's going on?" Mike asked, his gaze darting between Carly and his brother.

She had no intention of explaining anything to the man who hadn't seen fit to tell her the truth. Even as he'd spouted all the reasons she shouldn't marry Peter, he hadn't revealed the most important one of all.

"Ask your two-timing brother." Suddenly exhausted, she leaned against the wall once more. "I'll handle notifying the guests and the caterers and returning gifts."

The small office felt suffocating. She walked around Mike, ignoring his burning gaze. She'd reached the door when she paused in midstride and glanced at Peter. He looked stricken, but at this moment Carly couldn't bring herself to care. Nor could she bring herself to reassure him about his partnership. Before finding out about his affair, she'd made sure her decision wouldn't affect her father's feelings about Peter.

"One more thing."

"Yes?" he asked warily.

"Take this." She twisted her engagement ring off her finger and smacked it into his hand before turning on her heel and storming out of the room.

* * *

Mike started to sprint after Carly, but Peter's strong grip on his arm halted his departure. He pivoted and came face-to-face with his brother.

"What?" Mike asked. He didn't want to waste time dealing with Pete.

"The truth. Did you tell her?" For the first time, his composed brother looked shaken.

Though Mike wished he could pity him, the one person he felt for was Carly. "I wish I'd had that honor. Not telling her is something I'll have to live with." He prayed it wasn't too late. "Obviously she's brighter than you thought."

Peter groaned, bracing a hand on the doorknob. "No, I'm just a hell of a lot dumber."

Mike shook his head. "When will you learn, Pete? Things have a way of coming back to haunt you."

But he needed to speak to Carly, and unless the elevators were slow, she'd had enough of a head start for her to disappear into the crowd. By the time he'd reached the street, the clouds that had looked threatening earlier had erupted in rain showers. In this weather, finding an empty taxi would be damn difficult if not impossible.

He glanced to his right and relief kicked into him. Carly stood on a corner flagging down a cab. He ran, reaching the taxi just as she pulled the car door shut. He rapped on the glass and called her name.

She rolled down the window. "Go away." Her face was wet with moisture, making it impossible for him to distinguish between raindrops and tears.

"No." He reached for the handle and opened the door.

She promptly slammed it closed again.

"Have a heart, Carly. It's wet out here."

She glared through the half-opened window.

"Have a heart? That's a joke coming from you." She smacked her hand down on the inside panel.

He reached for the handle before she could lock the cab door. This time he was prepared for her resistance. His strength was no match for hers and the door flew open wide.

Ignoring her murderous look, he flung his wet body into the seat, forcing her to move over or be crushed. She slid over quickly.

"Wise move," he said, shutting the door behind him.

Silence greeted him.

Leaning forward, he spoke to the driver. "Seventy-second and Second."

"Wait." She tapped the driver and the man turned to look over his shoulder.

"He's not going with me." Carly gestured toward Mike.

"The hell I'm not."

A wide grin encompassed the older man's face. "Me, I don't care where we go or how long we sit. The meter's running." He patted the metal box. As if on cue, the digital numbers increased.

"I'm in no rush." Mike shrugged and leaned back in his seat.

She groaned but remained silent. Raindrops pelted the windshield and the cabdriver began whistling.

Mike slicked back his hair with one hand. This was one battle of wills he couldn't afford to lose. He needed the chance to explain. More important, Carly needed to be with someone who cared.

He glanced at his watch. The meter ticked off another fare increase. The driver switched tunes. Over the off-key whistling, Mike heard a clicking sound and turned. Carly huddled in the corner, arms wrapped around herself, shivering, her teeth chattering. She pushed her wet bangs out of her eyes with one hand before wrapping her arms around her wet body once more.

He muttered a harsh curse and repeated her address aloud.

The driver looked at Carly. "Miss?"

"Just go," Mike said through clenched teeth.

The man glanced over his shoulder at Carly again and she nodded. He swiveled back in his seat and placed the car in gear, jamming his foot down on the accelerator.

Mike looked at Carly and held out his arms.

"Either you've lost your mind or your ego is bigger

than I thought." She curled into a tighter ball.

He let out a groan, reached over and pulled her into his embrace. She tried to squirm free, but he held on tight. "Save your energy to argue with me later," he said. "Right now we're both wet and freezing. If you don't want to come down with pneumonia, take advantage of my body heat."

Heaven knew he was taking advantage of hers. Every breath brought with it her unique scent, and her soft body had begun to relax, molding to his.

"I'm only doing this to keep warm," she mumbled.

He chuckled. "I know."

"I'm still angry."

He leaned his chin on the top of her head. "I know that, too." And a confrontation was sure to follow.

* * *

After towel-drying her hair, Carly wrapped herself in an ivory terry-cloth robe. The hot shower had warmed her body but not her heart. She felt ice cold inside. Ironically, heartache wasn't the problem.

She'd already broken up with Peter, already accepted that caring couldn't replace love when he'd blundered into his admission. And though he'd shocked her, Mike's silence hurt worse than anything Peter had done. Her ex-fiancé had merely wounded her pride and convinced her that she'd been going through life with blinders on, in more ways than one. She pulled the lapels of the lace collar together at her throat, drew a deep breath and stepped out of the bathroom.

Mike stood in front of the credenza that provided a makeshift bar. He'd changed out of his wet clothes. He wore the large gray sweats she'd lent him, a towel draped around his neck... and nothing else. Her gaze was drawn to the muscles in his back and upper arms.

The strength in his body seemed as prevalent as the strength in his character. Another misguided perception, she thought. He, too, had betrayed her.

The rational part of her rebelled at the notion. The emotional part, the part that had been humiliated tonight, clung to the possibility. A confrontation with Mike was inevitable. Today's encounters were like a flood after a lifetime drought.

He turned, drinks in hand. "Here." He held out a brandy snifter. "I think we could both use this to warm up."

After accepting the glass, she walked away from him. "You knew."

"Yes."

She admired his honesty. She just wished it had come sooner. Carly closed her eyes and inhaled deeply. How could the confirmation of something she'd already known hurt so much? She pushed up the sleeves of the oversized robe. "That's something, I suppose."

"What is?"

"At least you didn't lie this time."

He grasped her arm and swung her toward him. His eyes bore into hers. "I never lied to you."

The heat of his fingertips seared her skin, branding her and making it difficult to remain focused. "What would you call it?" she asked. "A tiny omission?"

"Yes." With a groan, he released her. "Put yourself in my position. Where would you find yourself?"

In the middle, she silently conceded.

"I did the only thing I could. I pushed with the knowledge you already had and hoped you'd come to the right decision."

"And if I hadn't?"

Guilt etched his features. "I hadn't thought that far. I guess I had faith in you. And besides... I couldn't bring myself to be the one to hurt you."

"And you didn't want to betray your brother." A tear trickled down her cheek. She wiped it away with the back of her hand.

"That, too."

She lifted her drink to her lips with trembling hands. "Where did you find this stuff?" Carly only used the credenza when she entertained or had friends over to hang out. Brandy wasn't a staple in her liquor cabinet. She stifled a laugh. She didn't have a liquor cabinet.

"I dug through your kitchen and managed to come up with something we could use. Drink up. It should help relax you."

She took a sip. The dark liquid burned a path down her chest yet centered her somehow. She crossed the room and stared out the window to the street below. Carly tried to hold on to her anger at Mike. She had to. Without it, she didn't have anyone to turn the brunt of her feelings upon. So he had been torn between her and his brother. His brother, his only family, or a woman he'd just met. Not much of a decision there, she thought bitterly.

He walked toward her and placed a hand on her arm. "Do you understand what I'm saying?" His intense gaze bore into hers, causing a pulse-pounding heaviness in her chest.

Afraid she understood him *too* well, Carly backed off, heading for the center of the room, searching for space.

SIX

Mike watched Carly's retreat. Somehow she seemed too composed for a woman who had not only broken her engagement, but just discovered that her fiancé had been cheating on her as well. She set down her drink on the hardwood floor and turned her attention to a white wicker basket overflowing with magazines. She crouched down, knees resting on two over-sized throw pillows fringed in yellow.

As he watched, she began rummaging through the stack of magazines, tossing unwanted ones to the side. A huge pile formed beside her. Whether her task enabled her to ignore him or whether she was searching for something, he couldn't say. The relevance of her actions escaped him, but she seemed to need the distraction.

Her movements caused her robe to part, revealing a hint of cleavage and the round swell of one breast. Mike sucked in a deep breath but found it impossible to look away. He shifted positions and lowered himself onto the couch because if she looked up now, she'd run far and fast. The sweats she had lent him were too tight under ordinary circumstances. What he felt now went way beyond ordinary.

He glanced at her again. "What are you…"

"Aha. Found it." She rose, then ripped a page from the chosen magazine. "Did you know there's such a thing as wedding insurance? Damage control for a wedding canceled due to unforeseeable events. Let's see." She skimmed the article in her hand.

Mike narrowed his eyes and focused on her distracted behavior. He realized now that she was more affected than he'd originally thought. He fought the urge to ease her pain. To wrap her in his arms and never let go.

Just because she'd dumped his brother didn't make her ready for another relationship. Especially a short-term affair with a man who, as she'd so rightly said, was unable to commit. Whose career was destined to take him farther away at any time.

She'd had enough pain. He had no desire to add to it.

She raised her gaze from the magazine page. "Too bad," she murmured. "Weddings canceled because the bride wore blinders while the groom was a cheating son of a bitch aren't covered." Her voice broke over her words. As she lowered her arm to her side, the page drifted to the floor.

"Carly…" Mike stood.

"It'll cost every penny I have in savings and then some to cover the expense of ending this charade."

"Peter will pay his share," Mike muttered. He'd see to it. "Better now than after the ceremony."

She attempted to laugh, but choked on a sob instead. She dropped to her knees and bowed her head. Her damp hair fell forward, obscuring her face from view. Without warning, her shoulders began to shake violently.

Something inside him shattered at the sight. Not since his parents' deaths had he allowed another person to get close. As tight as they were, not even his brother had breached the wall around his heart. Carly tapped into emotions he'd never experienced before, ones he didn't understand now. She'd reached the part of him that he'd protected for the better part of his life. Watching her, he had the unsettling notion that nothing would ever be the same again.

Mike crossed the room and crouched down beside her. He lifted his hand and then let it drop uselessly to his side. Never having received a warm or loving embrace as a child, he wasn't sure how to comfort her now. He only knew he had to try.

He wrapped his arms around her. Her body molded to his. She rocked back and forth in his embrace as he held on tight. The fragrant smell of her shampoo drifted around him, tickling his nose, tempting his restraint.

As need surfaced, comfort became a hazy notion. He coaxed her back until they lay side by side against the pillows on the floor. Mike cradled her head, running his fingers through her silken hair. Gradually, her trembling subsided, but she didn't push him away. They lay together in silence. Her rapid breathing slowed. As she unconsciously matched her breaths to his, a feeling of contentment stole over him. It was as if he'd been running away and had finally found what he'd been searching for.

"Want to talk about it?"

"No." The muffled sound was almost lost. With one hand, he brushed the tangled hair off her face.

"I'm sure it hurts to be betrayed by someone you love."

She shook her head. "I wasn't."

Wasn't what? he wondered. *Betrayed?* Because if Peter had done nothing else, he had betrayed both her trust and her innocence. Mike hoped he hadn't destroyed them as well.

She drew an unsteady breath. A glassy sheen coated her eyes and her dark lashes were fringed with moisture. "I wasn't betrayed by someone I loved," she said, lowering her gaze. "I compromised until there was almost nothing left of me. In being so accepting, I gave him the freedom to cheat on me." She sighed. "In a way, I deserve *some* of what I got."

"How the hell can you think that?"

"I didn't say I deserved all of it, but there's no escaping the fact that I used him, too." Looking down, she stared at her hands. "I never loved Peter."

Mike exhaled long and slow. He hadn't known how badly he'd needed to have his suspicions confirmed until now.

"But at the very least I thought he was the kind of man to honor his commitments the way I'd planned to honor mine."

Mike wanted to defend his brother. To insist that he was sure Peter *meant* to be faithful. But the truth was, Peter looked out for Peter first. Carly had never factored into the equation. He hadn't intended to hurt her, but he hadn't stopped to think about her before jumping into bed with his new associate, either. "If it makes you feel any better, he took me by surprise, too."

Her smile seemed forced. "It doesn't matter. I was so wrong. As long as things seemed right on the surface, I convinced myself I was happy. But I wasn't." She shifted positions, rotating her legs until she sat Indian-style beside him. Her robe ended below her knees, revealing toned calves and long legs. "I was dead inside and just never knew it. Until you, Peter was safe."

"And I'm not." Mike raised his hand to the back of her neck and brushed aside her hair.

"No." Her lips parted. "You're not."

"Why?" He massaged her muscles that had worked themselves into tight knots. Her skin felt smooth and soft beneath his hands.

"There was no..." She spread her hands in front of her. "No..."

"Passion." He ventured an educated guess. One based on the fact that she hadn't slept with his brother, had never seemed to want more from Peter than a passing touch. But mostly he based his knowledge on instinct.

Startled, she jerked her head up. "How..."

"Did I know?"

She nodded.

He grinned at the shocked expression on her face as he completed her sentence for the second time. "Because you couldn't feel an emotional pull toward my brother and respond to me like this."

He leaned over and brushed his lips over hers. His hand, already at her nape, dug farther into her hair as he shifted positions and slid his tongue across her lips. She sighed aloud.

He meant to coax her into understanding but there was no need. Instead of pulling away as he'd expected, she raised her hands to his face and opened her mouth beneath his.

The kiss was hot, intense and like nothing in his previous experience. Although he had intended to prove a point, he lost track of everything but Carly.

He lifted his head and looked into her soft brown eyes.

"Mike." His name was a plea he couldn't resist. He captured her lips again. Together they tumbled backward onto the floor. He trapped her slender body between his legs and shifted until the heat of his arousal was pressed firmly at the juncture of her thighs.

Pausing long enough to open his eyes, he watched her face as he further inflamed her senses. He ground his hips against hers.

Her eyes glazed over. "More."

He grit his teeth against the combination of pleasure and pain and thrust himself against her welcoming body. She uttered a sigh and rotated her hips, causing him to curse the barrier of clothing that separated them. Then he closed his eyes and pushed deeper.

His mouth never left hers, his tongue mimicking the erotic motion of their bodies. She rocked beneath him and wrapped her arms around his waist, pulling him closer. Their bodies fit together as one.

Still separated by layers of clothing, they were both

close to losing control. Mike hadn't touched an inch of her skin, yet he ached to lose himself inside her. The thought amazed him. After everything she'd been through, she still... His mind cleared in an instant. His body, however, refused to cooperate and throbbed with unsatisfied need.

He gentled his kiss in an effort to bring them down from the peak they'd almost reached. He wanted Carly, but on equal terms. With her needing him as much as he needed her. Giving and receiving comfort wasn't a solid basis for making love.

He allowed himself one last lingering kiss before pulling himself up and away from her soft, willing body.

* * *

Seconds passed before Carly's passion-fogged mind cleared. Two things became evident at once. She'd succumbed to the heat of desire, to the point of almost making love on her living-room floor. And she wasn't the one who'd called a halt.

Her entire body throbbed. Need pulsed through her, but she drew a ragged breath and forced herself to relax. She looked at Mike. His head rested on bended knee and he studied her with a pensive expression. His golden eyes betrayed none of his inner thoughts. She didn't have to be a mind reader to know them.

Carly recognized Mike's withdrawal for what it was—another rejection in a day fraught with them. She might have been the one to break things off with Peter, but in admitting his affair, he'd all but rejected her, declaring her worthless in his eyes.

She had the sinking notion that no one would ever love her enough to put her first. Her father hadn't cared enough to put his family before his mistress. Her fiancé had always given his career and lover higher priority. And Mike, the one person with whom she'd felt a solid connection, had rejected her twice. First by keeping silent and, again, by pushing her away.

And she would have slept with him anyway. Embarrassment flooded her, cooling her passion faster than an icy shower. "I'm sorry," she said, standing as she spoke. "But congratulations. You proved your point. I couldn't have been in love with Peter and I have no self-restraint when it comes to you." A lot that said about her moral fiber, she thought.

Mike groaned. "That wasn't the point I was trying to prove." He leaned back, propping himself up on both elbows.

"Why else pull back? Heaven knows I wouldn't have stopped you." Self-loathing filled her voice, directed at both her actions and the question she'd just voiced. He didn't need to know that his rejection bothered her.

"What happened just now"—he gestured back and forth between them—"that was about you and me. No one else was in the room. No one else was between us."

"I know," she whispered, remembering the way she had writhed beneath him. The shame of her wanton response burned inside her.

"Don't look at me like that," Mike said in a husky voice.

"Like what?" Turning from the heat of his stare, she attempted to straighten her rumpled robe.

"Like you're afraid of me."

"I'm not."

"Aren't you?"

She shook her head. "I'm afraid of what you make me feel," she admitted. *Afraid of who you make me become.*

"Don't be. Because the next time will make this one pale in comparison, I promise." His eyes raked over her body. Beneath his heated gaze she felt naked and exposed.

He rose at a leisurely pace, a man comfortable with himself and his sexuality.

"There won't be a next time." She tightened the sash around her waist, turned and stepped back before he could crowd her personal space.

But he anticipated her reaction and grabbed for the material of her robe. He pulled her backward until she leaned against the hard contours of his body. "Yes, there will. But next time you'll want *me*, not just comfort." His warm breath fanned her ear.

If he only knew how much she wanted him... even more than she'd sought solace in his arms. But she closed her eyes and let his words sink in.

He assumed there'd be a next time. Because she'd been eager and willing, despite his betrayal, he'd assumed all was forgiven. Carly didn't know who she was more furious with, Mike or herself.

Because she wanted to believe in him. Wanted to trust that he desired more from her than just hot sex. Though it couldn't change things between them, she needed to believe they shared more than just passion. Because when that passion flared, a living, breathing monster came alive. It brought the past to life and caused her to doubt the present.

He pressed a gentle kiss against her neck. She trembled against the feather-light touch. "Just go, Mike."

"Will you be all right?" he asked, obviously resigned.

She nodded.

"I thought so." He gathered his damp clothing from the floor. "You're strong, Carly Wexler," he said before disappearing into her bathroom.

"But not strong enough to resist you," she murmured to the empty room. She leaned against the nearest wall, closed her eyes and forced air into her lungs. She couldn't resist the man whose omission had hurt her more than her fiancé's affair. She shook her head and breathed in deeply once more. No sooner had she drawn another breath than the bathroom door swung wide open.

"What are your plans now that you're officially unengaged?" he asked. He'd changed back into his damp jeans and working boots. His black T-shirt clung to his broad shoulders and back.

"Are you sure you want to go home like that?"

He grinned. "It's either the wet look or I leave half-naked and barefoot. Your choice."

When he focused his smile on her, nothing else in the world mattered. She could almost forgive him for anything. "Go with the wet look. The neighbors don't need a free show." But *go*, she thought silently.

"Well?" he asked.

"What?"

"Your plans."

Obviously she couldn't get rid of him easily. If he sensed her need to be alone, he didn't show it. She hadn't had a chance to give her future much thought. But perhaps now that she had the time, as well as her freedom, she ought to try. "I really don't know. I need to get away." The truth surprised her, as much as the fact that she'd spoken the words aloud.

"Anyplace special?"

No place she'd share with him, but she had an idea in mind. Someplace where she could be alone to learn about herself and what *she* wanted out of life. A place far from Mike and his charismatic influence, she thought. "No destination in mind," she said, forcing a smile.

"One minute you're planning a wedding, the next a vacation. You go with the flow. I like that in a woman."

Until today, her rigid schedules and plans had ruled her life and kept her sane. She was on a wild free fall now and had no idea where she would land. The thought frightened her. He might like that carefree way of life, but she didn't.

He closed the gap between them and reached out a hand to touch her shoulder. She shook her head. "I'm okay." His touch would be her undoing. Both emotionally and physically she wasn't strong enough to resist him right now. She needed to keep her distance.

"I know." He lowered his hand to the side. "How will you keep busy?" he asked, as if understanding that she needed a mundane subject change.

"School is out, my column is in reruns and I'd planned on using the summer to write my book. I can work anywhere with a computer." She fingered her still damp bangs.

"Maybe someplace with a beach," she said, thinking aloud.

"Sounds therapeutic." He spoke as though his mind had escaped elsewhere.

"True. My life has just been thrown a curve. A vacation might get it back on track."

"Makes sense."

She nodded.

He offered no response.

An uncomfortable silence surrounded them. She glanced at him, her gaze drawn to the taut muscles in his arm, then the wide expanse of his chest. In her mind, she was back on the floor, Mike's firm body pressed against hers. This time, her lips tasted bare skin.

He cleared his throat.

She blinked and her eyes met his. Amusement etched his features. A wide smile told her she'd been caught. She raised her hands to her flaming cheeks.

The safest move would be to get him out of her apartment. Once he left, he'd be out of her life. And she refused to analyze her feelings on *that* subject just yet.

She walked past him and headed toward the door. His footsteps sounded behind her. She placed her hand on the doorknob and turned.

"I can take a hint, however subtle."

She turned toward him. "Good. Then no hard feelings and good night."

"Get some rest and try not to dwell on anything too upsetting." He grasped her hand in his, entwined their fingers and caressed her palm with his thumb.

What should have been a casual gesture heated her senses. A flicker of warmth began deep inside and radiated throughout her body. Through sheer force of will, she didn't pull away.

He brushed her knuckles with his lips. " 'Night Carly. Sleep tight."

He might as well have said *dream of me*, since she doubted she'd do anything else. " 'Night, Mike."

She shut the door behind him, knowing in her heart that it was for the last time.

* * *

Mike knew he was taking unfair advantage. He knew Carly wanted to be alone. Yet he sensed deep pain beneath the surface, hurt that went way beyond a broken engagement. And he believed that pain could be traced back in time. Although he couldn't be the man in her future—he had too many scars of his own and a lifestyle she couldn't understand or accept—he wanted to be the one to help her heal and move on.

He'd deal with his own pain of losing her later,

when he'd pulled his life together and was back wandering the globe on assignment. He knocked and let himself into her father's office. Roger Wexler rose from his desk. "Good to see you, Mike."

"I appreciate you fitting me in, Mr. Wexler." He shook the older man's hand.

"Roger. And it's no problem. What can I do for you?" He gestured to the chair in front of his desk and waited for Mike to sit before lowering himself back into his own seat.

"Carly mentioned she was going on vacation. The beach sounds like a good place to recuperate." Mike was acting on a hunch, but he had no other leads.

Roger nodded and leaned forward on his elbows. "Sure is. We've spent a month at that beach house every summer for the past twelve years or so." The man's eyes narrowed, his curiosity evident. "Why?"

Mike wondered how much to reveal. Gazing into the older man's eyes, he opted for the truth. Too much in the way of lies had passed between this man and Mike's family. "One reason is a photo layout I'm doing for a local paper. I need a place to stay while I research the area and take some pictures."

"And the other reason?"

Mike cleared his throat. "Your daughter." Uncomfortable with the topic of conversation, he pushed himself up from his chair. He paced the plush office, admiring the view and the furnishings.

Despite the fact that this man was a lawyer, his office held a warmth that surprised him. The place reminded Mike of Carly. She obviously had more in common with her father than he'd realized. More than she wanted to admit.

"I see," Roger said.

Did he? Did the older man understand how Mike felt about his daughter, or did he put him in the same category as his brother? Mike shoved a hand beneath his blazer, into the back pocket of his jeans.

"Mr. Wexler..." Mike paused. How did one overcome the sins of one's brother? And did he have that right considering his intentions were good but not long-term?

Roger rose and met him in the center of the large room. "I'm not going to judge you based on Peter. And in case he didn't tell you, I'm not going to judge his work based on his action toward Carly."

"I haven't spoken to Pete." Mike had left the apartment early each morning and returned late at night. Until he'd come to terms with what his brother had become, he wasn't ready to deal with him. At least not yet.

"Well, I was all set to toss him the hell out. Until Carly begged me not to mix business with her personal life."

Mike should have been surprised, but he wasn't. Carly was too sweet for her own good. He met Roger's assessing stare. Brown eyes, the same warm eyes he'd looked into last night, stared back at him.

"He'll have to work hard to keep his partnership. And right or wrong, I'll be watching him. One slip and I'll do everything in my power to have his partnership revoked."

The older man let out a sigh, one that seemed old and overdue in years. "Whatever else I may have done, I do love my daughter."

"I believe that, sir."

Roger nodded. "Back to you. You went after her last night. Is she okay?"

He obviously hadn't heard anything personal from Carly. The thought saddened Mike. And something in Roger's tone caught Mike's attention. Called to him, in fact. He'd bet the question hadn't been an easy one for the older man to ask.

"As well as can be expected," Mike said. "She's hurt. Feels betrayed." He shook his head.

"She's known too much of that."

"I wouldn't know, sir." Mike thought the older man deserved to know that Carly had kept family secrets buried.

Her father walked over to a group of framed photos on his desk. Picking up one in a small silver frame, he frowned. "Too damn much," he muttered.

Mike didn't know what else to say. Asking for an explanation felt like prying. Although he now realized the person who hadn't put Carly's needs first, was her father.

"May I?" Mike reached out a hand.

Roger nodded. Enclosed in the small frame was a family photo of a younger Carly and her parents. Mike placed her age somewhere in her early teens.

Since he hadn't come from a typical family unit, family dynamics was unfamiliar terrain. But his years as a photographer had taught him to judge a picture by the body language of the subjects. Against the backdrop of a beach house and the ocean behind it, Roger stood, his hands at his sides. His wife leaned away from him, one hand around his waist, the other on her daughter's shoulder. Carly smiled for the camera, but her expressive eyes betrayed an inner unhappiness. This photo displayed the family Mike had seen at dinner the other night. Had things once been different?

"Nice," he said, handing the picture back to the older man.

Roger shook his head. "Some things in life you can't undo," he murmured, obviously caught in another time. He cleared his throat. "Well. You said you need a place to stay in the Hamptons."

Bingo. "Yes. I figured you're familiar with the area. Hotel, motel, whatever. Nothing fancy."

In silence, Roger studied him through narrowed eyes. Finally he spoke. "Okay." He walked over to his desk, pulled a sheet of paper from a Lucite tray before grabbing a pen and beginning to scribble. "Here's a list of decently priced hotels and motels near the beach."

Grateful, Mike reached across the desk and accepted the paper, fingering it between his thumb and forefinger. "I appreciate it."

"Good. There's something you can do for me in return."

"Name it."

"Don't hurt my daughter." Rounding the corner of the desk, Roger eased himself into his chair.

Uneasy, Mike shifted his stance. "We're friends and I think she could use one right about now." Mike didn't want the older man misinterpreting his long-term intentions toward Carly. He was only around to help her through a rough patch in her life, not to be a part of it later on. His gut twisted painfully.

"I think you're right. And she won't take comfort from me or her mother. I'm glad someone else cares enough to give it to her."

After he and Roger talked a little longer and the older man had given him additional beach information, Mike rose from his seat. He shook Roger's hand and walked into the hall.

He paused, debating the merits of speaking with his brother. His own anger hadn't yet subsided. Any discussion would only widen the rift between them. He'd deal with Pete before he left the States, but not now.

As he headed for the bank of elevators, the burden of Roger's words weighed heavily. The older man trusted him despite the actions of his brother. He trusted him with his only daughter.

But Mike couldn't live up to that trust. Not completely. Because though Mike wanted to be with Carly, to help her through the rough times, he knew he couldn't... *wouldn't* be there for the long haul.

Carly Phillips

SEVEN

Carly let herself in to the meticulously clean beach house. Nothing had changed since her parents first bought the place over ten years ago. The white cabinets and Wedgwood blue trim gave the illusion of a cheerful home. Growing up, knowing the farce her parents lived, Carly had found this room depressing.

Not so today. The house hadn't changed. Had she? Since the purpose of this vacation was self-discovery, she was about to find out. She'd taken care of ending her engagement, returning gifts and notifying friends and family before arriving, enabling her to come with an upbeat attitude. The airy kitchen, skylights and bright decor genuinely pleased her. The ringing of her cell phone brought her out of her musings.

Her mother's voice greeted her. "I just wanted to make sure you got there okay."

"I'm fine, Mom. I just walked in a little while ago."

The phone call shouldn't have surprised her, but it did. A while had passed since she'd turned to her mother for anything. Only now did Carly realize that her mother hadn't stopped trying. Carly had stopped accepting anything from Anne. Another thing she'd have to try and resolve on this solitary trip.

"I'm sure. I'm fine. Yes, he offered to pay for all the wedding expenses, but I broke things off and I want to cover my share." She and Peter had conversed via voicemails and somehow managed to undo all the arrangements.

As her mother spoke, Carly got yet another glimpse into Anne Wexler's way of dealing with life: grin and bear it. "Yes, I know people are talking at Dad's office. I assumed they would. Gossip's gossip. But I really don't care and you shouldn't either. Would you prefer I'd have gone through with it and been miserable for the rest of my life?" *Like you?*

"I'm sorry, Mom. Really. Can we just drop the whole thing? I appreciate you checking on me and I'll call you in a few days."

The doorbell rang. "Got to run. Talk to you soon. 'Bye."

Only after she'd hung up did Carly realize that her head had begun to pound. "Be right there," she called toward the front door.

She grabbed for two aspirin in her bag and a glass of water before answering the door. Just because her mother had opted to continue in her marriage didn't mean Carly wanted to deal with things the same way.

Her entire life she'd walked a fine line, fearful of repeating both of her parents' mistakes—her father's search for more love and passion and her mother's blasé acceptance of all obstacles thrown in her way. Because her father's errors were so much more damaging, she'd unbelievably come within weeks of turning into a replica of her mother.

She was still petrified of becoming her father's daughter—the last interlude with Mike proved she was on the brink—but still, at some point she'd lost track of Carly and what *she* wanted out of life. And that was something else she'd have to look into. With her seniors' graduation behind her and the whole summer ahead of her, she could focus on herself.

The doorbell rang again. She headed into the hall. A door led to a small entryway and landing where a long staircase connected the upstairs and downstairs portions of the house. She swung the door open wide.

"Can I borrow a cup of sugar? I'm all out."

"Oh, no."

Mike grinned. "Yup. So how about that sugar, Sugar?"

"Couldn't you think of something more original?" she asked.

"Avon calling?" He advanced two steps.

Carly forced herself to remain in place. Any retreat would give him too much information about how much he affected her. Like he needed anything more than her overly enthusiastic response the last time they were together, she thought, her cheeks burning at the memory.

She shook her head. "Try again."

"How about this?" He took another two steps forward and met her lips with his in a scorching kiss. His mouth moved over hers with such skill and perfection, she was surprised her legs still supported her. All she could do was reach for his shoulders and hold on.

The kiss was all she'd dreamed about and everything she'd missed. It was also too short. He freed her with an agonized groan, but his golden eyes still glittered with desire.

She pushed her bangs out of her eyes and exhaled. A frustrated sigh escaped instead. Apparently her plans for solitude and self-learning were about to be drastically altered. "What are you doing here?" she asked. Forget about how he'd found her. She wasn't sure she wanted to know.

Mike shrugged and walked past her into the foyer. "Well?"

"I've got two answers to that. Work and you."

She narrowed her eyes. "Explain the work part."

Once in the kitchen, he turned a chair around and straddled it with his legs. Muscular legs, she noted before shifting her gaze to his face. She chose a chair opposite him.

"I'm doing a layout for a special on summer vacation spots," he said.

"Right. The man who loves travel and danger suddenly chooses the Hamptons. Hoping to expose the ever-present beach pickpockets?"

"Watch the sarcasm," he said with a grin.

"Then try the truth." She stood and walked to the refrigerator. She pulled out a can of soda and popped the top. "Cola?" She offered the can to him, hating the ingrained politeness that governed her actions. She wanted to toss him out before she could succumb again. The good girl in her didn't know how.

He shook his head.

She downed a large sip of soda herself.

"I'm here to work. And to see you," he said.

The bubbles burned her throat, causing her eyes to water.

"To make sure you have a friend if you need one, or a shoulder to cry on if it comes to that."

She coughed, wiping tears from her eyes. Damn his sense of chivalry, anyway. It made turning him away that much more difficult. "Well, I appreciate the sentiment, but there's no need." She slammed the soda can on the table for emphasis. The liquid popped up, splashing over the oak surface. She shot him a frustrated glance and grabbed for a towel to wipe up the mess.

Propping his elbows on the table, he sat in silence.

"What, nothing to say?"

"Why should I bother? Obviously you believe what you're saying, or you're trying to convince yourself." He shrugged. "I happen to know better."

"You're certainly full of yourself today."

He grinned. "It's part of my charm."

"I'm serious, Mike."

"So am I. I know you want to believe you don't need anyone, but it isn't true. No man... er, woman, is an island," he said with a grin.

She narrowed her eyes. "I see. So last time you ran into trouble, you turned to... who?"

"The psychologist in you," he muttered. "I respect that even if it makes my life more difficult. This isn't about me."

She shrugged. "Maybe it should be."

"Stalemate, sweetheart." Rising from the chair, he reversed positions and slid it under the table before starting across the kitchen.

"Where are you going?"

He turned. "I made this my first stop. I have to find a hotel."

"You mean you don't have a reservation?" she asked warily.

"Not yet. This assignment came up at the last minute."

"I'll just bet it did." She forced a grin. "Good luck." And he'd need it. A sunny weekend at the Hamptons. Just where did the man think he was going to find a hotel with a vacancy? Or a motel? Or even a rat-trap dive?

Carly swallowed a rising tide of anxiety. Maybe he'd get lucky. He'd better… or she'd find herself in deeper trouble than she'd ever imagined.

*   *   *

Hours later, Carly sat on the deck watching dusk fall. Dark clouds had rolled in over the horizon and thunder rumbled in the distance. She curled up her knees and wrapped her arms around her legs, letting the beauty and anger of nature rise around her. Despite the pending storm, she felt a measure of peace. By this time, Mike had to have found a room or he'd have returned. Though she knew he wouldn't make himself scarce for however long he planned to stay, at least she still had a measure of time to herself.

A cool breeze slid over her skin as the wind picked up in intensity. She shut her eyes and sighed with contentment. This trip away from home and her problems had been the perfect solution. Surely here she'd find the missing pieces in her life, the reasons she'd nearly married a man she knew she didn't love. The reasons she'd turned a blind eye to what she now viewed as his obvious betrayal. And the reasons she was so drawn to Mike, the antithesis of everything she'd ever believed she wanted in a man.

A lone drop of rain fell onto her arm. She wouldn't be able to sit here much longer. The storm would drive her in.

"I should have known stupidity ran in my family."

Carly opened her eyes. Mike stood before her, frustration evident in both his voice and the aggravation marring his expression.

"Not a hotel room to be found?" she asked in a sugary sweet voice.

"You knew."

She sighed. "Let's just say I figured."

"And I should have, too." He glanced at the sky. "Want to go in?"

A fine mist had begun to rain down, but Carly wasn't ready to head inside yet. Not when it meant she'd be enclosed in the small, cozy house with Mike.

She shook her head. "The drive back shouldn't be too bad. It's against traffic."

He raised an eyebrow. "No can do. I told you, I'm here to work."

"So you plan to stay where? In your car?" She fingered her bangs. They weren't soaking wet, but they were on their way.

*　　*　　*

"I'll make do." He studied her with those mesmerizing eyes until she felt he could read her mind and decipher her heart's desire. No, she didn't want him in her house. No, she didn't want him sleeping in the next room. How could she, when she'd proven she couldn't trust herself around him? Couldn't trust the wanton person she became?

"Make do how?" she asked.

Mike didn't answer. He wasn't sure where he was headed. But no way could he stay and torture her any more than she was torturing herself. He hadn't thought beyond renting a car and driving out to find her. Roger hadn't mentioned the booked hotel rooms. If Mike had been thinking, he would have realized it himself. But that was the problem. With Carly occupying his mind, other thoughts didn't exist.

He reached out and grabbed for her hand. "You take care of yourself, okay?" He squeezed once and let go, then made for the steps leading to the beach.

"Mike, wait."

He turned. "What?"

"Come back. Please. You deserve an explanation."

He walked toward her. His sneakers squeaked against the wooden planks. "You sure you don't want to take this inside?"

"Not yet. Just sit, okay?"

He joined her near a lounge chair and waited.

"I'm... afraid," she admitted softly.

Mike knelt down next to her and reached for her hand. Her skin felt cold and clammy and he realized she wasn't exaggerating. "You don't have a monopoly on fear, Carly."

He looked into her eyes. The emotions churning inside her caused her brown eyes to appear darker than usual. "How can you talk about fear? You drop into danger-filled situations for a photograph. What can possibly frighten you?"

"More than you can imagine." He'd witnessed children being orphaned like himself. He'd left in mid-assignment and violated every professional code by which he lived. Those realities were hard enough, but the fears he had been referring to had nothing to do with his past or his career. They had everything to do with Carly.

He traced the veins in her slender wrist with his thumb. She dropped her gaze. The wildly erratic beat of her pulse moved him in ways he failed to comprehend. And therein lay the source of his fear.

"I'm afraid you'll throw me out without us ever having had the chance to explore what's between us." Raising her hand, he kissed the throbbing pulse point in her wrist. "And I'm afraid you'll let me stay and I'll lose part of myself to you." Worse, he knew. Even if he stuck around now, he'd take off when the call came, leaving her stranded and alone. Hurt again. No matter how good his personal reasons, he'd create a mess he had no idea how to undo.

Startled eyes met his and he laughed. "Welcome to the club," she said.

"What frightens you?" he asked.

"The feelings between us."

He nodded in silent acknowledgment. Until recently he'd believed her fear was grounded in guilt over Peter. Without a ring binding her to another man, that theory no longer applied. Which meant something more was at work, something more held her back from Mike.

"And," she continued, "the fact that no matter how torn you were, you betrayed me. You spent days on end with me, knowing Peter was cheating. Knowing I was sacrificing to make him happy when he wasn't doing nearly the same thing for me. I trusted him. I trusted you. And I'm not sure what that says about my judgment, all things considered."

"I tried every which way short of outright betraying my brother to let you know you were making a mistake. When you're ready, you'll know that's true. But since you're not, I'll be going."

She rolled her eyes. "Where? To sleep in your car, or were you planning to pitch a tent?"

"I've made do in worse and you know it."

"But not while I was consumed with guilt. There's a guest room," she muttered, just as the skies seemed to open wide and a torrential downpour began.

She ran for the house and Mike followed, ducking under the rolltop awning and through the sliding glass doors. Once inside, she grabbed for two towels in a hall closet and tossed one his way. They dried off in silence, Mike refusing to glance at her wet T-shirt or tousled hair, tossed by the wind.

He also refused to contemplate his motives. He could have gotten into his car and driven the long ride home. Instead he'd checked out the last motel and U-turned it back here. He glanced over.

"I'll take you up on that room," he said at last. He purposely didn't say for how long. Both knew he couldn't stay.

* * *

Carly nodded. So he was staying. It wouldn't be for long, she knew. She raised her gaze. "I'll make up the room."

"I'd appreciate that."

"I hope you realize you won," she said, unable to control her words. She couldn't help feeling as if she'd been set up with this trip of his.

"No, Carly. We win," he said quietly. "We share something special, and no matter how temporary my stay is, we're good for each other."

Unexpected tears filled her eyes as he spoke. Swallowing over the lump in her throat, she forced out equal amounts of honesty. "There's something you should know."

"I intend to know everything about you."

He retrieved her hand and she trembled under the heat of his strong touch.

"You're an experiment for me," she said.

He looked amused. "How's that?"

"I need to see if I can resist this pull between us."

"Why would you want to?" Lines creased his forehead in confusion. She resisted the urge to reassure him by smoothing them with her fingertips.

"Do you think there's such a thing as too much passion?" she asked instead, ignoring his question. "Feeling things too deeply?" She nibbled on her lower lip and watched him.

His face grew serious as he pondered her question. "Not unless the passion controls you," he said at last.

She clutched his hand tighter. "Explain that." She desperately needed to understand.

He was right. They were good for each other in many ways. But it was that sexual pull she couldn't understand. Her views in life were skewed by what she'd seen growing up. So much that she wondered if she'd ever get past it.

He lifted his free hand to twirl a stray lock of her hair between his thumb and forefinger. "In a healthy situation, passion may overwhelm you, but you know when and how to hold it in check." He treated her to a sexy grin. "And when to let go."

"And in an unhealthy situation?"

"It takes over areas of your life where it doesn't belong. Passion becomes a destructive force." He wiggled her fingers until she'd released her death grip on his hand.

She glanced down at the deep grooves her fingernails had etched in his skin. "Sorry," she murmured, running her hands over his bruised flesh.

"What's this all about?" he asked.

She shrugged, unable and unwilling to answer.

"Okay. But I've got a question of my own."

"What?" she asked.

"Did you get engaged to Peter because there was no passion or in spite of it?"

Without looking at him, she answered, "I think you know."

"Carly." He lifted her chin. His hazel eyes glittered with gold flecks and banked desire. When he spoke, he never took his gaze from hers. "Passion and love are healthy human emotions." He ran the pad of his thumb over her lower lip.

The pull reached down to her inner core, the words *passion* and *love* colliding in her brain.

"Whoever taught you differently?" he asked.

Two tears ran down her cheeks.

"When you're ready to talk about it, I hope you'll come to me." Leaning toward her, he kissed the teardrops away.

*   *   *

Mike walked the stretch of private beach behind the Cape house. Barefoot, the sand felt cool beneath his feet. With the sun barely up over the horizon, the ground hadn't yet warmed and was still brisk from the evening chill.

He asked himself again what he was doing here. The question had haunted him for the past three days. Three days in which Carly had treated him like a guest she either ran into or didn't. He'd allowed her the privacy, ignoring the closeness of the small house even as he'd listened to her toss and turn in the next room at night. During the day, he used the time to roam the public beaches and capture tourist shots for the newspaper. At night he paced the floors, wondering how much longer the reprieve would last.

He owed his colleagues more than a wave goodbye

and a simple "see you later," and his boss wouldn't put up with much more of Mike's silent routine. Beyond calling with a phone number, Mike had deliberately stayed out of touch. Because once he had to return abroad, he would hurt Carly as badly, if not worse, than his brother had. Not that she'd asked a damn thing from him. She didn't have to. One glance at those bottomless eyes accomplished the same thing. He'd do anything for her.

Except leave her alone. If he left without testing those powerful feelings, he'd lose something precious. A less selfish man would walk away before she got hurt.

"Hi."

Startled, he turned. "I didn't hear you." But he was glad she'd sought him out on her own.

"Not too tough to sneak up on someone on the beach." She held her sandals over one shoulder. "Bare feet." She wiggled her toes for emphasis. Her pink nails stood out in sharp contrast to the beige sand.

"Someone's in a good mood this morning," he noted and wondered why. "Have you changed your mind about letting me hang around?"

She shook her head. "Hit the kitchen around seven. I'll treat you to a real feast."

She'd managed to shock him. "What did you have in mind?" he asked.

"It's a surprise." With that, she whirled and ran toward the house.

Mike took off after her. Catching up with her was easy, wrapping his arms around her waist and bringing her down on top of him easier still. To his never-ending surprise, she didn't resist or try to pull away. She lay in the V of his legs, breathing hard from her run and laughing at the same time. Her face was flushed pink and her carefree smile told him that she'd left her problems behind, at least for now.

Lying beneath her sent a jolt of awareness through his system. Her soft laughter caused her body to move against him and he couldn't hide his instant reaction. He wanted her.

He knew the exact moment she realized their intimate position and his state of arousal. The joyful laughter ended and her expression clouded. She braced her arms and rolled off to the side.

As difficult as it was, he let her go. There was much he still didn't understand, but he recognized her fear. For whatever reason, the intense attraction between them caused her to pull back. He sensed the only way to reassure her was to prove they could control the passion. Easier said than done, he thought. He drew deep breaths, trying to concentrate on the waves crashing against the shore instead of Carly's ragged breathing. Proof she wanted him, too.

*   *   *

In silence, they lay on their backs and stared at the wide expanse of sky. White puffy clouds dotted an otherwise clear blue backdrop.

"Beautiful," she murmured.

He glanced over at her. "Sure is."

"Mike?"

"Hmm?"

"What's it like dropping into the world's hot spots?"

He stiffened. Her choice of topic surprised him, but he couldn't bring himself to be anything but honest with her. "Exciting."

"Dangerous?" Carly asked. Because the thought of Mike in the center of some war-torn country or worse sent goose bumps chasing along her skin.

"Sometimes."

She wondered how she'd feel, knowing he was putting himself in danger, not knowing if he'd make it back home alive and in one piece. She shivered from the sudden chill. He drew her close, probably mistaking the impact of her turbulent emotions for a reaction to the cool ocean breeze.

Her head lay in the crook of his shoulder and she savored the closeness they'd found on an emotional level. "Why do it?" she asked.

"It's not for the glory or the thrill of cheating

death, though there are some guys who feel that way." His warm breath fanned her hair. "I'm not sure exactly, but I like knowing I've made a difference. That maybe one picture prevented someone somewhere from starving to death or being killed."

Aid those in need. Did he realize how similar his goals were to her own? "Sort of like the reason for my column."

"How so?"

She didn't realize she'd spoken aloud. "So many kids have no one to talk to. I hope at least one person is able to make a tough choice because someone cared enough to listen."

During the worst period of her life, no one had been there for her. No one had listened. Her mother had refused to discuss the tragedy or the impact on their lives, leaving a teenager to cope alone. She couldn't turn to her obviously grieving father, and besides, her anger at him wouldn't allow her to. She hoped some teenager used her column to vent feelings he didn't feel free to express at home.

"We're some pair." He chuckled aloud. "We sound like avenging angels."

"I'm no angel. I'm just making sure no kid thinks he has to go it alone."

"Like you did?"

Carly pushed herself to a sitting position and

stared. She wanted to lash out, to shout at him. *Stop finishing my sentences. Stop reading my mind.* He was getting too close and it frightened her. "How…"

"Educated guess."

Obviously she was easy to read. Mike brushed the grains of sand from her back. After this roll in the sand, she'd need another shower. Unwilling to drop the subject, at least until she learned what she wanted from him, Carly glanced over. "So what are your reasons for playing the Good Samaritan role?" Some deep, dark secret like her own? she wondered.

"Nothing I haven't already told you. When you grow up without, you tend to overcompensate. This latest escapade with Pete drove that point home."

At the mention of her ex-fiancé's name, she waited for the pain of betrayal to surface. It never came. Relief, pure and sweet, flooded her. "How so?" she asked Mike.

"He thinks money and power will make up for all he missed. He doesn't realize that material wealth won't replace love."

Why had he chosen that particular word? She whipped her head around expecting to meet his potent gaze. Instead, Mike was staring out at the ocean, one hand rubbing his right shoulder hard.

She studied him. His muscled physique created waves of longing, but what did she feel for this man that was so different than anything she'd ever experienced? Was it to be savored as something special or feared as an extension of her father's legacy? It was about time she found out.

Her future was at stake.

"So Peter's looking for money and power to make him happy." Which cemented what she'd already known—the reasons why he'd gotten and remained engaged to her. "But what are you looking for?" she asked Mike. "All the travel, the danger—are you running?" she asked softly.

He didn't respond.

She placed a hand on his arm. "I think you are." Which made them very much the same, Carly thought sadly. "The question is, when will you stop?" *When would she?*

He remained silent. The answer was locked inside him, she thought. And like her, he'd have to face his private demons. Sooner or later.

* * *

Mike stood in the entryway to Carly's kitchen, eavesdropping on his chef for the evening. She stood, hands on her hips, staring into an oversized lobster pot.

"Call me a coward, but I can't do it." She brushed her bangs off her forehead with her fingers.

He grinned as she glanced from the wriggling lobster on the counter to the boiling pot on the stove. "Can't do what?" he asked.

"Drop live lobsters in there. I thought I could, but I can't."

Mike glanced at the counter where two lobsters moved languidly in plastic bags. "Dinner?"

"Only if we boil them alive."

He chuckled. "Why don't you go outside for a while? I can handle things in here."

She glanced into the steaming pot. "They scream."

"What?"

"When I was younger I went to a friend's house for dinner. Her older brother took a lot of pleasure in informing us that if you listen carefully you can hear their high-pitched screams before they die." She shuddered.

"You don't believe that."

"Not anymore, but I did. I was ten. I had nightmares for weeks."

"Boys can be cruel."

"Yeah. So can men," she said.

"I'll give you that." He leaned over and kissed her soft cheek, then gave her a playful swat on the behind. "I'll handle this."

"I owe you one."

He met her gaze. "And I fully intend to collect."

She turned for one last look into the lobster pot. Mike snuck up behind her, wrapping his arms around her waist and burying his face in the expanse of skin at her neck. Her vanilla-like scent was permanently etched in his dreams. Reality was much sweeter.

She stiffened at his initial touch but relaxed against his insistent nuzzling at her ear. His hands splayed across her stomach. Every ounce of willpower he possessed went into keeping them below the round swell of her breasts. He pressed his lower body into her back and was greeted by her soft moan of pleasure in response.

He wanted to turn her around and bury himself inside her. He wanted to see her face when he entered her heat for the first time. He wanted all those things and more. But he didn't deserve them. Not when he couldn't give her all she so obviously needed.

He wanted to step back but needed her warmth and closeness for a minute more. Then he'd let her go. A yellow gauze dress ended above her knees and her bare back had turned a deep bronze courtesy of the sun. Her skin felt warm and welcoming to his touch.

He steeled himself to back off, but she turned. Any progress he'd made dissolved like a sand castle under a crushing wave. Eyes glazed and face flushed with desire, she looked disoriented and unsteady. He reached out a hand to support her and immediately noticed that her nipples were drawn tight beneath the flimsy fabric.

Without conscious thought he brushed one distended peak with his thumb. She swayed toward him, and damned if her knees didn't almost buckle. Control deserted him, and all good intentions along with it. Any thoughts he'd had of restraint vanished. He knelt down and replaced his hand with his mouth, suckling her through the material of her dress. She braced herself by grasping the handle of the stove.

He bit down lightly. She murmured his name at the same time her legs gave out completely. Mike reached for her, supporting her until she was able to stand on her own.

"You're a hazard in the kitchen," she said in a husky voice.

"Look who's talking. Dress like that and expect results." He laughed and she joined him. For the first time she didn't pull back or appear to mentally berate herself for her desire. Progress? A start? Or just an aberration? he wondered.

She pointed to the large metal pot. "You have lobsters to cook," she said in an unsteady voice.

"Then get going... before I get distracted again."

* * *

Carly didn't miss the desire in his gaze and opted to

bolt for the deck. She kept herself busy setting the table, opening a bottle of wine and contemplating the wisdom of inviting Mike for dinner. She'd convinced herself she could get to know him without any complications. He'd been in the kitchen all of thirty seconds and common sense had deserted her.

The last time, in her apartment, she'd been devastated by the fact that when she should have been seeking comfort, she'd only felt desire. Now while seeking to prove to herself that she could exert self-control, it all but deserted her.

What would happen if she gave in? a little voice in her head asked. Gave herself over to Mike, to passion, to all the emotions she'd taught herself to fear? The answer came easily and without thought. She'd fall in love... if she hadn't already. And then what?

The man had a penchant for travel and danger. He wasn't the type to settle down, and even if she could get past the fear of their explosive chemistry, she wanted someone who would put her first. How could she love a man who might never make it home? How could she have the safe family she wanted, or subject children to his kind of unstable life? No, she thought sadly, their future just didn't exist.

She deliberately ignored the shaft of pain the thought caused, attributing it to hunger. "How long does it take to boil the damn lobsters anyway?" she muttered aloud.

*   *   *

Carly picked up the nutcracker and attempted to tackle a large lobster claw. The shell cracked. Mike's startled laugh surprised her, and she looked up to find him wiping water from his face with a paper napkin.

"You squirted me." He grinned.

"Sorry." She licked freshly drawn butter off her fingers and stared at the large claw on her plate. "I forgot lobster's like spaghetti. It's a no-no on the first date."

"So is corn on the cob." With a grin, he took a large bite. "So it's a good thing this isn't a first date." He waved the corn in the air as he spoke. "We're way beyond first impressions, remember?"

She leaned back in her chair and swirled the wine in her goblet. "What were your first impressions, anyway?"

He rested on one elbow and turned to study her. "I thought you were sexy as hell and I wanted you," he said in a low, steady voice.

"Oh." She felt her lips move, heard her response, but her brain had ceased to function. Her body, on the other hand, leapt to life. Every nerve ending tingled in delicious anticipation of his touch. Even her breasts felt unnaturally heavy. She waited for him to reach for her.

Instead he asked, "What were your first impressions?" The gold flecks in his eyes danced with delight, in obvious anticipation of her response.

"I thought the police ought to do a better job of patrolling the city streets," she said, treating him to one of her sweetest smiles. After all, his rugged charm *had* nearly sent her running in the opposite direction.

Before she could gloat over her comeback, his arm reached out and his hand grasped her wrist, pulling her close. The warmth of his touch seared her skin. "Didn't anyone ever teach you what happens to women with smart mouths?" His face was inches from hers.

"No. Why don't you show me?" The wine had dulled her more rational self and replaced it with a courage she didn't ordinarily possess. Nothing else explained such bold, wanton behavior, especially in light of her self-revelations earlier. But those revelations had served another purpose besides shedding light on the future. They'd made her realize she couldn't give up the present. It was all they had.

Her eyelids fluttered closed and he slanted his mouth across hers. He kissed her softly, gently. She had expected the hot intensity of their past encounters. His tenderness caught her off guard.

Nothing could have surprised her more than the reverent way he caressed her mouth. He wet her lips with his tongue, then rubbed his own against hers, soaking up the moisture. He created a damp path down the side of her neck and up to her ear, where he paused and nibbled the lobe with his teeth. As if from a distance, she heard her own satisfied moan.

The cool ocean air hit wet areas of skin and she shivered. His thumb traveled the same path as his lips, drying the moisture and warming her at the same time. The gentleness of the gesture shocked her, causing a lump to form deep in her throat.

She drew a deep breath and waited for the sensual onslaught to continue. His fingers merely traced the outline of her mouth. She opened her eyes to find herself staring into his. Her body felt alive with need. She ached for him, yet a part of her knew she should call a halt to this now. It wasn't too late.

Nervously she ran her tongue over her lips, coming into contact with the rough pad of his thumb. His skin tasted salty and warm, making her wonder what other tastes and textures awaited her. She wanted Mike with a depth of feeling that surpassed mere passion. As she contemplated those rampant emotions, she feared she had been wrong. Perhaps it was too late. For a lot of things.

Slowly, he removed his hand from her soft lips. "When you said feast, you weren't kidding." He pointed to the table. With difficulty, Mike changed the topic to more mundane issues. Like food.

*   *   *

Her forehead creased in confusion and she fingered her bangs in the nervous gesture he'd come to anticipate and enjoy at the same time. Mike stilled her hand with his and groaned. He'd had no choice but to stop. Every time he kissed her, her honest, open response startled him. When they made love—and he didn't kid himself that it might not happen—he wanted her acceptance to be made knowingly. Not in the throes of passion. After his glimpse into her innermost fears, he owed her at least that.

"You liked the dinner?" she finally asked, regaining her composure.

"Loved it. I can't remember the last time someone cooked for me."

"As it turned out, you did the cooking."

"Yeah, but only because their screams of pain didn't bother me."

He winked and she tossed a paper napkin at him. "Chicken," he teased.

"Maybe." She shrugged and began clearing the table. With his help, Carly collected the plates and extra food and carried everything into the kitchen. She looked at the pile of dishes in the sink and sighed. "The perils of eating in."

"Now that everything's inside, can cleanup wait?" he asked.

"I guess so. Why?"

"You up for a walk on the beach?" Mike extended one hand, silently asking her to meet him halfway. They might take that stroll on the beach, but he wanted much more. He had little doubt she knew exactly how much.

Her brown eyes narrowed. He hoped she was searching her heart.

"As long as I don't end up rolling in sand again." Her full lips turned upward in a provocative grin. "It took me forever to get the sand out of my shorts."

"Okay. I promise you won't roll around in the sand." He met her gentle gaze. "But I can't promise you won't be rolling around somewhere... more comfortable."

He scanned her face for some positive sign. She smiled and placed her hand in his.

"I always had doubts about that beach scene in *From Here to Eternity*." She gave an exaggerated shudder. "All that sand and water. Hard to imagine how they maneuvered." She wrapped her fingers around his. "I'll bet there are plenty of rooms in this house that can accommodate us."

"Are you sure?" he asked.

She nodded. "I'm sure." From the hungry look in her eyes, he knew the walk on the beach would have to wait.

EIGHT

With her nerves stretched to the breaking point, Carly followed him into the bedroom in the back of the house. She gazed at the king-sized water bed in awe and trepidation. "This is incredible."

"Next best thing to the beach." Mike released her hand long enough to shut the bedside lamp.

With the shades open and the sun still in the process of setting, the room was cast into a dusky glow. Her gaze took in the unfamiliar space. Suddenly she was all too aware of the large bed.

"Did I give you too much time to think?" he asked, approaching her from behind. His hands brushed her hair off her shoulders as he placed a soft kiss on her neck.

She trembled and closed her eyes, heightening the pleasurable sensation. "Maybe."

The sound of his retreating footsteps was followed by the crush of leather as he sunk into the beanbag chair in the corner. Silence surrounded them, but she wasn't inclined to break it, not yet. She needed these precious minutes and he seemed to understand. She pushed back the hair from her face.

If she hadn't slept with her fiancé, why would she contemplate making love with Mike? She thought of his laugh, his smile, and the way he knew how to listen, then retreat without saying too much. He seemed to respect her feelings, even if he didn't comprehend the reasons behind them.

In the ensuing silence, she forced her mind to function, and the conclusions she reached were staggering. If she wasn't in love with him, she was well on her way. She knew the damage emotional involvement could cause, had avoided it this long. Especially with a man like him. So what now?

She swallowed hard and turned. In the shadows, she made out his masculine form reclining on the floor. A seagull screeched in the distance. Mike reached one hand toward her and waited.

She padded across the hardwood floor and stopped in front of him.

"I want you to know what you're getting into," he said.

Somewhere during the past few minutes her decision had been made. "I do," she whispered. They'd been moving toward this moment from the beginning. The outcome was as inevitable as the changing tide. She only hoped they didn't destroy each other in the process.

"I can't make any prom…"

She covered his lips with one finger. "I know."

Looking into her dark eyes, Mike believed her. The knowledge should have lifted an otherwise heavy burden. It didn't. What did he want from her? he wondered. Better yet, what could she expect from him? He hoped it wasn't more than he could give.

"Carly?"

She wet her lips. "I know these are a little outdated, but have you ever made love on a water bed before?" she asked in a husky voice.

Her velvety words wrapped themselves around him. She had apparently made peace with herself, leaving her reservations along with her inhibitions behind.

He shook his head in response.

"A first for both of us, then." She smiled and placed her hand in his. "I'm glad." After shifting her skirt, she knelt beside him and pulled him up from his seat on the floor.

He allowed himself to be led, only until he'd reached a standing position. Then he backed her toward the large bed that beckoned to them. When her calves reached the platform, he stopped and encircled her waist with his hands.

She smiled and lifted his shirt, her soft hands linking behind his back. He dipped his head toward her, but she caught him off guard. In one smooth motion she wrapped one leg around his and pulled him toward her so they tumbled backward onto the bed together. The mattress rocked beneath them in undulating waves. Carly landed beneath him, laughing with delight.

The tinkling sound and the light in her eyes removed whatever reservations had remained in his mind. "Think you're so clever?" he asked, brushing his lips over hers.

"Nope. I *know* I am." She smiled and laughed some more.

He kissed her again, letting her unique scent fill the empty spaces inside him. To keep from crushing her, he rolled to his side and propped himself up on one elbow. Sealing his mouth over hers, he entwined his tongue and feasted until he could barely breath.

They'd never done much more than this, yet each kiss contained more power than the last. He marveled at her ability to reach inside him with nothing more than a touch. What would happen when they came together? The conflagration would probably consume them both.

He wondered if that was the source of her fear, but before he could analyze further, her hand came between them and caressed his arousal through the rough denim of his jeans. His body jerked involuntarily at her touch and the bed swirled beneath them.

"When did you get so bold?" he asked.

"Only with you." Her hand cupped him tighter.

"Not yet." He removed her hand and grasped her fingers with his own. "Not if you want this to last."

"I want," she murmured. From beneath heavy lids, her eyes fastened on his face. He removed a strand of blonde hair from her cheek and kissed her lips.

"So do I." Reaching behind her neck, he opened the two buttons that held the top of her dress in place. He watched, mesmerized, as he drew the top down, inch by tantalizing inch. Since he'd been given a brief sample before dinner, he knew what lay beneath the light material.

The dress fell to her waist and he sucked in a deep breath. Carly, however, closed her eyes. A rosy color tinged her cheeks. He raised one hand to cup her face. "Hell of a time to get shy, sweetheart."

Personally she couldn't think of a better one. "Takes an awful long time for the sun to go down, doesn't it?" she asked, while silently praying for darkness. She raised her arms to cover herself, but he stopped her by grabbing hold of her wrists and pulling them down gently.

"Don't. I've been waiting too long." His voice sounded rough to her ears.

She allowed him to draw her arms to her sides, but kept her eyes tightly shut. Whatever she had anticipated, it wasn't this slow perusal. She no longer felt capable of lighthearted banter, not when she felt so vulnerable and exposed.

"Beautiful," he murmured, just before she felt wet heat on one breast. In shock, she opened her eyes to see him leaning over her, lavishing undivided attention on her hardened nipple. She gasped at the utter intimacy of the act. He suckled her, nipping and soothing with alternate breaths. Heat, which had begun in her chest, traveled with lightning speed to the juncture between her thighs.

Were these wonderful sensations the same ones she had feared hours earlier? Right now, she couldn't imagine why. She ran her fingers through his thick hair, enjoying the rasp of his day-old beard against the sensitive skin on her chest.

He lifted his head long enough to turn to the other breast, giving it equal attention. She felt only a moment of cool air on the spot his mouth had abandoned, before his hand began equally skillful maneuvers. Muscles in her stomach clenched as he rolled one nipple between his thumb and forefinger, while working the other with his mouth.

Unable to think, let alone feel embarrassment, she laid her head back on the pillow and gave herself up to sensation. She was only dimly aware when he lifted her up to release the back zipper of her dress, of when she raised her hips to help him remove the barrier between them. The bed shifted and swirled beneath them, causing her to giggle at more than one inopportune moment.

At some point, and she couldn't remember when, he'd shed his shirt, because her hands now buried themselves in the hair on his chest. He groaned as she worked her way outward. She smiled and licked each nipple in turn.

"Carly." He gasped her name, warning in his voice.

She blew cool air on his wet skin in response. With another groan, he grabbed her wrists and pinned her backward. The bed rocked beneath them. "You don't play fair."

She bat her eyelashes at him. "Was I supposed to?"

"Not if you don't mind me returning the favor." He paused for a hot, wet kiss, then made brief work of removing her lace panties. Together they got rid of his jeans and briefs. The bed wasn't nearly as cooperative, however, and he stood to complete the task.

Laughing, Carly grasped the purple cotton from his hands and dangled the briefs from her fingers. "I'd never figured you for plain white, but this?"

"I told you purple was my favorite." He bounced down next to her. "But I am glad you gave it some thought," he said with a grin.

She tossed them aside. "More than a little." Her hand circled his pulsing length. His sheer size stunned her and she gasped aloud.

"I would never hurt you."

She lowered her gaze. "I know. It's just that I've never…"

"I know." He silenced her and eased her embarrassment with a kiss before reaching for the night-table drawer. "Help me," he said, handing her the foil packet.

With shaking hands, she complied. Never had she thought of protection as an erotic act. In the future, she'd never think of it as anything else.

Her fears had long since evaporated under his gentleness. He'd touched a place deep inside her. More than her body was involved in the act that was to come. Much more.

He straddled her with muscular legs. His erection nudged at her, barely easing the throbbing ache of desire. She lifted her hips and he eased into her slowly at first and then harder, pushing inside with one hard thrust. She gasped at the initial shock of pain.

"I'm sorry."

She shook her head. He had nothing to be sorry for. He waited, poised above her. She felt him deep inside her. Mike filled her body but also her heart. She knew it the same way she knew nothing in her life would ever be the same. He paused to kiss her, working his tongue in her mouth as if searching for something greater than both of them.

He began to move inside her, and soon his gentle movements weren't enough. She wanted him deeper, wanted more from him than she'd ever dreamed possible.

The bed rocked in time with their movements, making it difficult for Mike to take things slowly. She enclosed him in her warmth, making them both fight against feelings so intense, they thought they might drown. She murmured his name and wrapped her long legs around his waist, forcing him as hard and as deep as he could reach.

She contracted around him and cried out. Any control that Mike had maintained shattered along with her. Surging into her, he drove higher. Mike let go, losing himself inside of her the same way she was lost in him...the way they both wanted – and feared – that they would.

* * *

Carly lay in Mike's arms, but sleep eluded her. She listened to his deep breathing and cuddled closer to his warmth. She tried not to think about anything but the miracle of them being together, but reality intruded.

Eventually, she would have to deal with their parting. She pressed a kiss against the back of his warm hand and tried to sleep.

She came awake with a start. Mike's body had stiffened and his arms tightened around her until breathing became next to impossible. His own breaths came in short gulps and he groaned. She felt the sheen of perspiration covering his body and realized he was in the throes of a violent nightmare. Should she wake him, or let the dream run its course?

"Mike?" She tried to turn, but his arms constricted her movement. "Mike?" she said, louder this time.

Abruptly he released her. With difficulty, she drew deep breaths and rolled toward him. He looked in her direction and turned away.

Her heart thudded painfully in her chest as she realized that he intended to shut her out. "I can't help if you won't talk to me," she said, drawing the sheet up over her bare chest. "Trust me." She placed a hand on his still clammy skin.

"Seems to me I told you the same thing a little while ago. You didn't open up." With his back to her, his words sounded all the more harsh and accusing.

"My mistake," she admitted.

He seemed not to hear. "You don't trust me, why shouldn't I return the favor?"

His words hit her like a blast of cold air, but she

forced herself to remain rational, to let the professional part of her look in. She recognized his pain and as a trained psychologist realized he was lashing out at the only available person. It didn't make his accusations hurt less, but she cared enough to take the brunt of his anger and direct it toward helping him heal.

"You're wrong, Mike. If I didn't trust you, we wouldn't be here now."

He ran shaking fingers through his already disheveled hair. "It's not something you want to know." He swung his legs over the bed and stood, oblivious to his state of undress.

She allowed herself a moment to drink in the sight of his naked body before grounding her thoughts. "If it affects you, I need to know. But I'm not what's important now. You are, and you need to talk. Whatever it is, I can handle it."

He stood at the window, gazing into the darkness. "My last assignment," he said at last. "Rather, my last uncompleted assignment."

"I don't understand."

"I'd hitched a ride back from the countryside with a guy in a Jeep. For a while we were the only ones on the road, but as we neared civilization, a bus pulled in front of us." His hands gripped the windowsill. "Must have made for a bigger target than a small Jeep, because mortar fire hit the back tires and sent the damn thing careening down the side of a ravine."

He paused, and Carly waited for him to continue. "I jumped out of my seat before the guy could stop. By the time I reached the bus, I heard the screams and smelled gas." His hand went to his shoulder and he worked the muscles with his fingers. Even from her distance on the bed, she could see how brutally he clutched at his arm.

She gripped the bedsheet, watching as he wrestled with the demons that plagued him.

"We knew we didn't have much time, but we had to get as many out as we could before the tank exploded. We pried open the bus door. Most of the people up front had taken a direct hit. They didn't make it." His voice shook, but he continued. "Most were women. In the end, we managed to pull a bunch of young kids from the bus and get them up the hill. When the explosion hit, I had one kid hanging from my neck screaming for his mother."

She swallowed, but the lump in her throat remained. And no matter how much she wanted to comfort Mike, the right words wouldn't come.

"I spent the next few weeks trying to track down this kid's father. Turns out he'd already been killed. The crash orphaned most of those kids."

Just like Mike. Oh, God. In a daze, she rose and walked up behind him, placing a hand on the shoulder he'd been abusing. "And this?" she asked softly. She stilled his hand beneath hers.

"Ripped open some muscle getting to the back of the bus."

She dropped a kiss on his shoulder, her lips coming in contact with new scar tissue. Why hadn't she noticed it earlier? "It must have been awful."

"Want to know the worst part? My damned boss was furious that I hadn't taken pictures. These kids just had their worlds ripped apart and he wanted exclusive photos." He shook his head in disgust. "Abandoned children and he wanted headlines."

"Mike…"

"But you know what? He was right. It was my job and I didn't do it. I couldn't. Any more than I could go back afterward." He dropped his head lower, leaning against the window. "All those kids…"

No wonder he was back in the States covering fluff topics like summer hot spots.

"Mike." She turned him toward her. In his tortured face, she saw how difficult the telling had been. Even worse was that he had lived alone with the pain all these months.

"Orphaned isn't the same as abandoned," she whispered. "There's a difference. Not much, I'll admit, but there is a difference."

"Tell that to those kids whose parents are gone."

He paused. "Forever."

Her heart broke for the little boy he had been. "Those parents didn't walk out on their kids. They were taken by a cruel twist of fate. That may not seem to make a difference now, but in the long run, the knowledge will ease the pain."

As she said the words, she recognized the irony. In the long run, for Mike, the distinction had meant little. "How long have you had these dreams?" she asked.

He shrugged. "Since the accident."

"I see." A period of hell, of equating his own situation with those of the children, of beating himself up for not getting hit instead, for not doing his job. What would it take to vanquish his demons?

The answer, she knew, lay in their parting. He had to return to the profession he loved and prove to himself that he could face his past and his present.

She didn't fit into the equation. Knowing Mike's strength of character, the separation would come much sooner than she had anticipated. He'd be doing her a favor, but right now it didn't feel like one.

"Running isn't the answer. You have to fight this." Even as she said the words, she knew she was pushing him away. Tears threatened and she closed her eyes against them.

"I know. I just don't know if I'm ready."

"You'll know when the time's right."

He nodded.

His hands cupped her face and he brought their lips together. He kissed her deeply, drawing from her both physically and emotionally until she was drained. She leaned into him, brushing her breasts against the hard planes of his chest.

"Carly." He groaned her name, then lifted her into his arms and carried her back to the bed. "Make me forget," he said as he entered her.

This time they came together in an explosive combination of want and need. He climaxed first and she followed. Their bodies entwined, Mike still inside her, she rested her head against his cheek.

When he whispered, "Don't leave me," she refused to believe the words, choosing instead to reassure him with a kiss.

* * *

The summer sun shining through the window woke Mike first. In the harsh light of day, last night's dreams were but distant shadows. Carly's long legs were entangled around his, reminding him that there was beauty in this harsh world.

She had been there for him, offering herself when he needed her. He had taken much more than he had been able to give. No one in his life had ever given of themselves, given at their own expense for his benefit.

His good mood this morning reflected the genuine concern he'd received during the night.

He stretched his arms over his head, letting his hand come to rest on her bare breast. It had been a long time since he'd felt so at peace. Perhaps he never had. And though reality tried to intrude, he forced it aside. He'd had little peace in his life. He wanted to enjoy it while he could.

Her brown eyes opened and she smiled.

"Morning." He placed a light kiss on her lips.

"Already?" She yawned. "Seems like we just went to sleep."

"I think we did, but there's always a way to make up for lack of sleep."

"How?"

Reaching for her, he said, "Spending the rest of the day in bed."

He wanted her again… as much as he wanted to avoid rehashing last night's nightmare. Whether she understood his dual need or not, he couldn't say. But she didn't argue. Instead she leaned over and kissed his lips, then playfully smacked at his wandering hand.

"Bed sounds good, but I can't put off my work any longer," she said.

"How much do you need to do today?"

"Well, I need to begin some sort of organizing for the book. And I need to sort through the letters that my editor forwarded for one or two new summer columns. I think one month of reruns is enough, don't you?"

"Not really. I could rerun last night with you over and over and never get bored." He brushed his fingers over her breast in a lazy circular motion. "What about you?"

Was it his imagination or did she stiffen at his touch. "I think we shouldn't go overboard." She grinned, but the smile seemed forced. "The work won't disappear, so I'm kicking you out."

Her backing off didn't surprise him and he decided to tread carefully. "Can't kick me out when I have nowhere to go," he reminded her, deliberately playing on her good nature.

"True. But I can bribe you to disappear for a while."

Her attempt at easy banter relaxed him somewhat, but he couldn't ignore the fact that she obviously needed to escape. And given her admitted fears, that need probably had more to do with their newly discovered intimacy and passion than with her need to work. Since making love had cemented an already strong bond, one *he'd* be forced to break, he decided to let her have her way.

"I'm a man easily bribed. What did you have in mind?"

"I'll make you breakfast and then you disappear for a few hours. Get lost. Go take pictures somewhere."

"Pancakes?" he asked. "You know you can't get pancakes in the places I've been hanging out lately."

"I think I can handle that," she said wryly.

"Bacon?"

"Okay."

"Fresh-squeezed orange juice?"

She grinned and poked him in the chest. "Now you're pushing your luck."

"Deal, then." With the subject off sex and onto food, Carly seemed completely at ease. Or did she just have him fooled? Before he left, the one thing he wanted more than anything was to help her get on with her life and put her painful past behind her.

"I'll get things started. Meet me in the kitchen in a few." She tossed off the covers and started to rise.

He reached for her, then changed his mind and let her go. Mike knew avoidance when he saw it. Hell, he was an expert on that subject. She'd helped draw him out last night. He owed her the same. Just because Carly had escaped his bed this morning didn't mean he'd let her elude her demons as well.

*　　*　　*

Carly removed the necessary breakfast ingredients

from the refrigerator. She didn't want to analyze how much she'd enjoyed waking up with Mike beside her, or how relaxing she found making breakfast and knowing he'd be there to share it. Neither one could last.

More than once, she stopped to pull down the blue oxford she had pilfered from Mike's closet. He had wrestled her for it, and of course, he had won. Which was why she now wore nothing beneath the denim shirt. She yanked at the hem, but it still only reached as far as midthigh.

Once she began the pancakes, she was grateful for the activity that took her mind off last night. Not only making love, but the revelations. Everything about the dark night had inadvertently served to strengthen the emotional bond between them.

She cared for him deeply. When he left her, she would be hurt in a way she hadn't believed possible. As much as she tried to convince herself that his departure was necessary for them both, the more time they spent together, the harder it was to believe.

Mike entered the kitchen to the delicious aroma of home cooking. The places he normally frequented lacked such a treat. Not only did the kitchen smell good, but it felt good, too. Too good, too comfortable. "I guess you can cook."

"You were worried? I should be insulted. Sit," she

commanded as she waved a spatula in his direction.

"Yes, ma'am." He grinned.

"Mike?"

"What?"

She glanced in his direction, a serious glint in her eyes. "You told me why you're in the Hamptons, but how'd you end up here? At the house?"

"On a hunch, I went to see your father at the office. I asked him for motel names."

"I see."

"He showed me a picture of your family. Taken here, I think."

She turned her head. Her expression was unreadable.

Mike pushed on. "He keeps it on his desk." The sound of oil in the frying pan drew their attention to the stove, and Carly turned to work on breakfast.

"Nice of him," she said. "I wonder if it reminds him of happier times." Sarcasm was evident in her voice. So was the hurt. Hurt he'd also seen in her father's eyes.

He recalled the photo and the pained look in Carly's young eyes. Happier times? He doubted it. He wanted to broach the subject without her declaring it off-limits. And maybe help her, as she'd helped him, to at least discuss the source of her fear. "He asked about you."

"What did you tell him?" She flipped three pancakes over and transferred them to a dish beside the stove.

"Nothing. But he was concerned."

Her snort of laughter seemed forced. "He'll get over it. He's still got his top associate, even if Peter won't be his son-in-law."

"Unfair, Carly. He told me he wanted to dump Peter on his partner-climbing ass. *You* talked him out of it. He seemed genuinely concerned about you, not Pete."

She had finished the pancakes and added bacon to the frying pan. Her jerky motions were at odds with the casual air of indifference she tried to maintain.

"Tell me about it," he urged.

Silence reigned until finally she spoke. "Remember what it was like being a kid?" she asked. "When life was one big illusion?"

"After my parents died, reality killed any hopes of that. Do you?" he asked.

"Yes. One day we were a happy family, no major problems that I knew of. The next, we're front-page news. Scandal of the year." She plucked the half-cooked bacon off the pan and stacked it next to the pancakes. He didn't see any reason to point that out. "Breakfast is served." She executed a mock curtsy and placed his dish before him.

"Thanks."

She smiled. "No problem. And because I like you, I caved in." Opening the refrigerator, she pulled out a large pitcher. "Freshly squeezed. Never say I don't accommodate you."

"Who me?" he asked. "Never."

He waited until she had seated herself across from him before continuing his questioning. "What kind of scandal?"

Her dark eyes met his, and though they beseeched him to drop the subject, he wanted her to unburden herself, to trust him enough to share her pain. "Well?"

"You should have been a cop," she muttered. "You never give up."

"I'm the next best thing to a journalist. What did you expect?"

She groaned and paused to eat something before beginning. "We lived in a small town in upstate New York. Everyone knew everyone else and gossip ran rampant. So when Roger Wexler, district attorney with political aspirations, hit the news, he did it in style."

She flicked her bangs out of her eyes and looked at him. He waited for her to continue in silence. "Want to take a guess?" she asked.

He shook his head.

"My dad carried on an affair with his secretary for one year. Until the woman forced him to choose between her and his family. In political terms, that's your lover or your career. Take your pick." She toyed with her pancakes, staring at the now cold stack.

"He chose your mother?" Mike asked.

"Yes, but that doesn't make the man a saint. I have no illusions that his decision was politically motivated. And I guess he thought his choice was the end of it."

"But it wasn't."

She shook her head, her pained gaze meeting his. "The woman killed herself, Mike. But not before leaving a suicide note and mailing it to the local paper. She was pregnant."

Mike sucked in a breath, wishing he had never forced Carly to resurrect these memories. But he had… "Then what?" he asked, knowing he had to hear the end.

"Life went on. Dad's political career was in ruins, but he never let it get him down. After a while, we packed up and moved to the city. Dad hooked up with some old law school buddies and started his own firm."

"What about you?"

"What about me?"

"How did all of this affect you?" he asked.

"I was fifteen. Your friends are your friends so long as there's nothing to laugh at. I went to school surrounded by gossip and laughter. I got used to it."

"I doubt that."

She shrugged. "Eventually we moved and I finished up in private school."

"But how'd you survive? Being a teenager is tough by definition. Add your problems…"

"I kept busy. Joined the teen crisis hot line. It kept me out of the house after school so I didn't have to go home where talk of our family problems was prohibited. I couldn't watch my mother pretend life was fine."

Bingo, Mike thought. Carly's problems weren't with her father alone. She resented her mother's behavior as well, and she'd closed them both out of her life. "So that's how you got started helping teenagers," Mike said.

She nodded. "I did similar work in college, majored in psychology, and eventually it translated into my column. End of boring story."

"You never forgave him, did you?" he asked, thinking of the distraught older man he had seen days earlier.

"Not in here." She placed a hand over her heart.

"Your mother did… or appears to."

"That's debatable. Mom's tough. She believes in handling your private pain in private. I got no support from her because she refused to admit we…" She gestured around the room, the house she'd visited as a child. "We, as a family, had a problem. I don't agree with how she chose to live her life, but I can't fault her for her coping mechanisms."

Mike disagreed. Carly blamed her mother every bit as much as her father but hadn't come to terms with her relationship with either one of them. But now wasn't the time to push her further.

"I'm not as big a person as my mother... you've seen that. She stuck by her man. I didn't stick with Peter. But my parents taught me one important lesson in life."

"And what's that?" he asked, sensing this was the key.

"I discovered firsthand what a destructive force passion can be and I'll never allow it to rule my life," she said with a vehemence that would have once shocked him.

But after experiencing her extreme reactions to their intense physical attraction, he now understood. She obviously believed she could separate their physical relationship from the emotional and thereby never repeat her father's mistakes.

He glanced across the table. Carly had begun clearing their half-eaten meal. When he had arrived in the Hamptons, Mike had feared he needed the safety Carly represented and not the woman herself. As he watched her clatter the plates into the sink, he realized how very wrong he had been. And how very much a part of him she had become. The truth frightened him almost as much as it obviously frightened her.

Carly turned from the sink with tears in her eyes.

He held out his arms and she sank into them. Burying his face in her hair, he comforted her the best he could and pushed aside all questions about the future.

NINE

After their emotional discussion, Carly tossed Mike out. Pushing the morning's events out of her mind, she set about organizing her columns into broad topics. Family, Friendships and Male-Female Relationships seemed like perfect headings, and hours later she had three distinct piles.

Family was a logical starting point but not a topic she was anxious to delve into yet. The same could be said of Male-Female Relationships, she thought, recalling her night with Mike. She set those piles aside. Friendship seemed like a safe place to begin. From there she would progress to Male-Female Relationships and ultimately Family Relations. The last two topics caused a distinct and unwelcome freezing in the region of her heart.

She sighed. How could she give advice when those areas of her own life were so complicated and unsettled? For years she'd walled off her emotions for fear of facing them. Thanks to Mike, she couldn't put off facing her personal life much longer. But first she had a deadline to meet. As a professional, she had learned to separate her personal feelings from her career. Anything less now and she would lose all objectivity.

She stood and stretched, each cramped muscle protesting her prolonged period of sitting in one position. The rumbling sounds of her stomach echoed in the empty room. This morning's breakfast had filled the garbage disposal more than it had her stomach. A late lunch would help, she decided, and headed for the kitchen.

The light tap on the side door startled her. This exit led not to the main drive but to the beach. She wasn't expecting company, and Mike wouldn't be so formal as to knock before announcing his presence. Pulling back the curtains, she found herself face-to-face with her ex-fiancé. He'd given her no warning and she found herself unprepared for any sort of confrontation.

"It was a long drive, Carly. Will you let me in?"

Stunned, she stared through the glass. "Sure." She opened the door and Peter walked into the kitchen. Dark circles surrounded his eyes and razor stubble covered his normally clean-shaven cheeks. He looked tired, she realized. And a lot more casual than the formality she'd grown accustomed to seeing. She took in his rumpled khaki chinos and a burgundy T-shirt and shook her head. She barely recognized him.

"This *was* a long drive." And he could have just used the telephone. "What are you doing here?" she asked.

He ran a hand through his neatly trimmed hair.

"I needed to straighten out a few things." His gaze traveled the length of her body.

Too late, she remembered that she wore nothing but the blue oxford shirt and a pair of satin bikinis. After her shower, the button-down had seemed like the most comfortable item of clothing to work in. And, she grudgingly admitted, after the morning's painful revelations, she took comfort in something that smelled so much like Mike.

Embarrassed by her lack of clothing, she retreated behind the center island and immediately felt more protected. "Everything already makes sense to me, so you wasted the trip." She didn't want to get into a discussion of why he'd felt the need to cheat on her with Regina. She already knew and didn't need to hear how she'd fallen short with him in the romance department.

Peter cleared his throat. "I think you have the wrong impression." He shook his head. "No, you probably have the right impression." He let out a groan.

"Let's make this easy. I've done a lot of thinking

since I've been here," Carly said. "We're both at fault. I certainly shouldn't have given in at every turn or let you think I was happy when I wasn't."

"And I shouldn't have…" He flushed, a deep red against pale skin.

"No, you shouldn't have." But she couldn't suppress a laugh. She much preferred being around Peter now that they were no longer engaged.

"I wanted to apologize in person. We were good friends once."

"I know." Her voice softened. "And I hope we will be again. We lost that somewhere along the line."

He shoved a hand into his front pocket and started across the kitchen. "We were good together for a while, and then… I stopped thinking about you and took advantage. Thanks for sticking up for me with Roger."

At least he'd admitted his mistakes. And maybe even learned from them. He deserved to be happy and she wished him the best, as long as it wasn't with her. "You're a good attorney. You never needed me as leverage."

He stepped up beside her.

"Nothing's happened to change your position… has it?" she asked, wondering if her father had acted out of belated parental concern.

"Actually, yes."

"I'm sorry. My father promised he'd be fair."

Peter grinned. "He was. You're looking at the newest litigation partner."

She breathed a sigh of relief. "That's great news."

His smile never reached his eyes. Instead he brushed a strand of hair off her cheek. "I never meant to hurt you." His hand came to rest on her shoulder.

She'd liked Peter, and he wasn't the only one who'd made mistakes. "I know that."

"Work time's over, Carly. Time for a little fun." Mike's deep chuckle and footsteps reverberated throughout the small house.

The sounds stopped abruptly. "I had no idea we had company."

"Mike…"

"I know you're my brother and she's your ex, but I'd appreciate it if you'd take your hands off her." The cool control in Mike's voice startled her.

Peter obeyed his command, releasing her immediately. No doubt it was the shock of Mike's sudden appearance that had him responding so quickly. Taking advantage, she took a few steps backward.

Peter's gaze ping-ponged from Carly to his brother. Mike stood, arms crossed over his bare chest. Fresh from a shower, his hair was damp and his jeans were zipped but unbuttoned. He looked settled and comfortable, a man who had a rightful place in her home.

The intimacy of the situation couldn't have escaped Peter. "Well," he said, "I see I'm not the only one who was fooled." The hurt in his voice was unmistakable. "While I was working, giving you free rein over my fiancé, you took advantage." He glared at his brother.

"It wasn't like that," Carly said, hoping to prevent irreparable harm between Mike and Peter.

"Are you telling me looks are deceiving?" He pinned her in place with a narrow stare.

"Yes." Carly glanced down at her bare legs. "I mean no." She threw up her hands in despair. "Nothing happened until after I got up here."

Peter laughed aloud. "I'm not that big a fool. At least you could have been honest about why you broke up with me." He turned toward Mike. "And you…"

Mike stepped toward his brother. "She's telling the truth."

"And why should I believe you?"

Mike groaned.

"Because he's your brother," Carly said. "And the only real family you have."

"Which is why he should have kept his damn hands to himself."

Carly drew a controlling breath. Until Mike, she had thought the devastating results of her father's affair spoiled the possibility of her enjoying a passionate, emotional relationship. He'd begun to make her believe otherwise, but she saw, now that she had been right all along.

She had succumbed to her feelings for Mike. They had crossed the line, and if he had jeopardized his fraternal relationship as a result she would never forgive herself.

"Talk," she pleaded, attempting to reach both brothers. "You're family. Nothing is more important than that. Especially not me." She gave Mike a lingering glance before walking out the door.

*   *   *

Mike watched Carly's retreating form. He was glad she had the sense to leave before that shirt lifted any higher. With one hand, he gave his brother a shove between the shoulder blades and pointed toward the kitchen table and chairs. "Sit."

Peter glared before answering. "I'm going. Relax," he muttered.

Mike settled himself in a chair and waited for Peter to join him, using the time to pull himself together. His brother had every right to feel angry, hurt and betrayed.

Mike's irrational jealousy the moment he'd seen Peter's hand on Carly's shoulder had only made a bad situation worse. He glanced at his brother. "She's right, you know."

"About what?"

"We're brothers," Mike said.

"That sure as hell didn't stop you from making a move," Peter said.

Mike slammed his hand on the table. "It sure as hell did!"

Stunned silence followed Mike's statement. He cursed his lack of tact, knowing he'd given his brother more information than he was probably ready to handle. Having an affair with another woman or not, ego was involved here as well as trust.

"You said you came up here on assignment." Peter waited.

Mike assumed his brother expected him to dispute that fact. "I am on assignment. Finished this morning." But Mike wasn't about to admit he'd handpicked the location of the assignment or the reason for his choice. "Look, Pete…"

"Forget it. From where I sit, things are pretty damn obvious. I'm just amazed I didn't see it sooner." Pete leaned back in his seat, not defeated but accepting.

"See what?"

"You really care for her." He shook his head, his expression one of pure amazement. "And all this time

I thought you were doing me a favor by hanging around her and helping her out."

"Of course I care about her, Pete." But he wasn't surprised that his brother hadn't known it. "You have tunnel vision. What's important to you and nothing else."

Pete had the grace to look ashamed. "I need to work on that."

Mike burst out laughing. He was surprised that his brother had bothered to drive up here, or to look deeper than his ego now. "Don't worry. There's hope for you."

Pete shot him a nasty glare. "Well, at least she's got you."

Mike didn't touch that statement because it would open up a discussion he didn't want to have with his brother. Whatever he felt for Carly, the emotion didn't change the course of his future. He couldn't expect her to rely on him if he couldn't rely on himself or the abilities he'd always trusted until recently. Nor could he expect her to accept a man who lived a transient life, one at odds with the stability she so obviously craved.

He looked at Peter. "If you'd really loved her or were marrying her for the right reasons, I'd never have... Hell, I should never have gotten involved anyway," he muttered.

Pete's smile was grim. "Neither one of us ever claimed to be a saint."

"But I should have come clean with you once she broke things off." But how could Mike have explained something to his brother that he hadn't understood himself? Things he still didn't have a firm grip on understanding.

"You know, I had a lot on my mind... the partnership decision, Regina, the ending of the engagement..."

Mike didn't miss the order of those things but chose to remain silent.

"You're right. You should have come clean. But you know something? It wouldn't have changed a damn thing. You'd have done what you wanted anyway. You always do." Pete laughed, breaking any lingering tension.

Mike relaxed. He and Pete would be fine. Carly was another story.

*　　*　　*

Mike jogged down to the beach and watched as Carly sat on the sand, gazing out at the waves crashing against the sandy shore. A light breeze blew her hair around her face. She had attempted to tie it back with a bandana, but the wind had destroyed the effort. As he neared the water, the smell of salt air tickled his nose. He'd miss the beach, he realized with a pang of regret.

He'd miss a lot of things. "Carly."

She turned at the sound of her name. "Hi."

"Hi."

She didn't smile. "Well, how'd it go?"

"Everything's fine. Back to normal."

She let out a sigh of obvious relief. "He came to apologize, and you know, I believe he meant it."

Mike sat down next to her.

"So you're on speaking terms again. I'd never forgive myself for coming between brothers."

"You are something special, sweetheart."

She blushed. Her face turned a shade deeper than the lobsters they'd shared. "Did I ever mention how much I like it when you blush?"

She laid her chin on bent knees. "You have a way of doing that to me."

"If you're talking about last night, I'd love to do it again." His hand came to rest on the back of her neck and he massaged the back of her skull with his thumb. But instead of relaxing, she grew stiff and unyielding beneath the innocent touch.

He swallowed a groan. He had an uphill battle ahead of him and he refused to draw back. Not because he wanted to sleep with her again, but because she had to learn that passion between two people could be a wonderful thing.

"So he really forgave us?" she asked.

"After cheating on you, he really can't pass judgment. And you two are over, remember? You didn't do anything wrong."

"Depends on your perspective. I can't believe we jumped into bed without ever considering the consequences. We should have given some thought to Peter's reaction before we jeopardized your relationship by getting involved. And the fact that we didn't is telling."

It sure was. Mike had no illusions. Carly's emotional withdrawal now wasn't aimed at protecting Peter, but herself. "Getting involved. Is that what you'd call it?"

"Yes. Wouldn't you?"

"Hell, no. We had sex. Isn't that what you're trying to say? A purely physical relationship, no strings, no ties, no caring involved."

She winced at his blunt description of what they'd shared, and at that moment Mike hated himself for hurting her. But he knew damn well what she was thinking. That by keeping their relationship on a purely sexual plane, she could equate it to her father's affair... and all the subsequent pain it had caused. Instead of facing what she felt for him, she'd run far and fast.

A part of him didn't blame her. He was no safer than his brother for her sense of security. He couldn't be the hearth-and-home kind of man she needed, yet he couldn't leave things alone. "Just sex," he said again. "Am I right?"

*   *   *

Carly licked at her dry lips. "Sounds reasonable to me." But it didn't. Hearing Mike's passionless, uncaring description of what they'd shared cut deep. Yet his words stated what she had forced herself to believe was the proper way to categorize their relationship. The safest way to avoid complications like this afternoon. The easiest way to let him go when he decided it was time to return to his nomadic, dangerous way of life. It was her heart that refused to cooperate and believe.

"Very generous of you." He leaned back on his elbows. "You know, Carly, you aren't fooling me."

"That's good, because I wasn't trying to."

"You're afraid to let yourself feel. So you label us with the one thing that scares you above all else, you beat yourself up for acting selfishly like your father and you run. Far and fast instead of facing the truth."

"Which is?" she asked, with pure sarcasm lacing her voice. "Since you know so much about running, you'd have to be right. So what truth is it that you think I'm afraid of?"

His hand cupped her chin and he met her gaze. "That if you look *us* in the eye, you'll see a lot more than just sex… and that scares you a hell of a lot more than a lust-filled relationship you can walk away from unscathed."

She jerked her face out of his grasp. "You're damn right it does. You're out of here at the first phone call, so why the hell should I look deeper? Why the hell should I let myself care?" Without waiting for an answer, she jumped to her feet.

Mike rose but remained silent. Obviously he knew he couldn't fight the truth.

With her vision blurred, Carly ran for the house. More than once she stumbled on the sand and rocks in her path, but she kept going. She flung open the door to the house. Feeling out of breath and desperate for peace from her rampaging emotions, she sought the security of home.

Instead she ran into Peter. "Just what I needed," she muttered under her breath. They might have resolved their issues, but he was the last person she wanted to see right then.

She wiped the tears still running down her cheeks with the back of her hand.

"Carly…"

"Not now, Peter. You apologized, I apologized.

Now let it be."

"I was just leaving." He glanced at her face and his brow furrowed. "You've been crying."

"It's been known to happen."

"Has it ever happened over me?" he asked.

She rolled her eyes. "For crying out loud, can we just…"

"I'll take that as a no. Whatever Mike said, just forgive him. It's obvious you care about each other."

She narrowed her eyes. "You figured that out based on the five minutes we all spent together in the kitchen?"

"We were friends before we made the mistake of getting engaged. I'd like to think I knew you pretty well. And I know that even though you broke up with me, what I did hurt you. Just remember one thing."

She swallowed hard. "What's that?"

"Mike isn't me."

"Thanks," she murmured, then attempted to duck around him.

"Carly, wait."

She sighed. "Make it quick."

His lips formed a wry smile. "I know my brother better than anyone. Everything he's done since he's been back proves one thing to me."

"What's that?" she asked, truly curious.

"He loves you. Think about that." Peter opened the side door leading to the beach then turned around to face her. "And if you ever need to talk, always remember that I'm still your friend, so you can call me or text me anytime." With a sigh of resignation, he slipped out, shutting the door behind him.

Carly stood in mute silence, Peter's words wrapping around her heart. Even if he was right, it couldn't make one bit of difference.

*   *   *

Carly spent the rest of the day in her room sorting through mail sent by her editor. Periodically, she would glance out the window only to discover Peter's rental car still parked on the street out front. Though she wondered when he would leave, she was glad Mike had time alone with his brother. As for her conversation with Mike, she preferred not to dwell on it for now.

She slit open a purple envelope and read the contents. The letter was brief and to the point.

I'm sixteen and pregnant. I haven't told anyone. I can't decide what to do and the problem is affecting every part of my life. I can't sleep, can't study for summer school, and no one has patience with my mood swings. Help.

Carly's answer was easy to formulate, but as this young girl would find out, even harder to carry through.

The first thing to do is seek medical attention, as prenatal care is of paramount importance. The next is to tell the people closest to you. Perhaps your parents, the baby's father, a teacher or local clergyman. If you don't talk, you can't expect to come to any meaningful decisions. Only after you face your fears will they seem less overwhelming. Then you can make the right decisions for yourself and your baby. Good luck.

Carly realized the irony in her answer. Talk out your answers. Face your fears. The one thing she advocated for this young girl was the one thing she hadn't been permitted to do. Talk. Perhaps if she had, she wouldn't be in such a sorry state now.

She finished punching the keys in the computer just as she heard a knock. After saving her document, she opened the door and glanced down the empty hall. But at her feet, she found a fast-food restaurant bag with a note taped to the brown parcel. "Be angry with me later. For now take the time to eat."

How could she be angry with Mike when he put her feelings first, always? She knew she had overreacted earlier, but with his leaving imminent, and his return as uncertain as their future, her nerves were on edge.

Inside the bag she discovered a large vanilla shake, a burger and fries. Apparently Mike had reworked the old adage, the way to a man's heart is through his stomach. He had certainly reached this woman's heart with his kind gesture.

Actually he had reached hers long before this. She munched on a french fry, pausing to lick the salt and grease off her fingers. She had decided not to fight the attraction for the short time they had left.

"Coast is clear." Mike's voice sounded through the bedroom door along with a loud knock. Startled, she glanced at her watch. Hours had passed. It was half past seven.

"Come in," she called without looking up.

*   *   *

"I thought Pete would never leave," Mike said. And if he hadn't threatened bodily harm, he might still be hanging around.

Carly didn't answer. She had changed into a flow-ered dress that wrapped around her body and reminded him of sunshine and happiness. Her head bent, she tapped away on her laptop computer keys. "I wasn't hiding out," she said at last, still without looking up.

"Could have fooled me." A quick glance around the room revealed piles of documents, reference books and the crumpled brown lunch bag. "You get a lot done today?" he asked.

She glanced up. "Pretty much." Her gaze darted

around the room, but she had yet to look him in the eye.

"Maybe I should have Pete come by more often. His presence seems to stimulate you."

"What?" Her startled gaze met his.

"Your mind," he said with a grin. "Stimulate your mind." He tapped his head and laughed. At least she'd finally looked him straight on.

"Oh."

She flushed, a reaction that inevitably reminded him of their first meeting. And their first kiss. Which led to even more intimate memories. "How was the burger?" he asked, more to distract himself than anything else.

"Greasy." Her face turned a darker shade of pink. "I mean good. Thanks for thinking of me."

He shrugged. "Not a problem. I'm always thinking of you." He crossed the room until he stood next to her.

Her eyes locked with his. Every time he looked into that brown-eyed gaze, her vulnerability hit him hard.

"I'm sorry about what happened earlier," she said. "I have no excuse and I apologize. We both know where things stand. I have no right to toss it back in your face."

He crouched down and took her hand in his. "Our

first fight is nothing to apologize for." His thumb methodically worked the pulse point in her wrist, massaging in slow but deliberate circles. When her pulse rate jumped, he smiled in satisfaction.

"Why not?"

"An occasional argument is a healthy sign. Any good psychologist knows that."

He raised his eyes in time to catch her grin and flick her tongue over her lips. Nervous energy radiated from her and he waited for the gesture he associated with Carly. Any minute now, he thought. She brushed her bangs out of her eyes. Bingo. He suppressed a laugh. Never having had such an emotional connection before, it still amazed him that he could read another person so well.

"Is that the only reason?" she asked.

"No."

"What's the other?" Her voice sounded unusually husky and he guessed she had figured out reason number two.

Their mental connection amazed him. "I'm not above relying on old standbys. Making up is half the fun." He tugged on her arm and yanked her toward him. She came forward fast, and together they toppled to the floor.

Carly landed on top of him in an indelicate sprawl. He brushed his mouth over hers.

"Mike." Her breath was as moist and sweet as his name on her lips.

"What?" he asked, trailing kisses along her jaw-line.

"Have you given any thought to when you'll…" Before she could voice the question that had been plaguing him, he silenced her with his lips. His tongue plunged into her warm mouth and he savored the heated sensation.

But even their intimate joining couldn't stop the remnants of her question from nagging at him. *Have you given any thought to when you'll be leaving?* The notion was almost more than he could bear. He would go because he had to… but not without leaving a part of himself behind.

Surprising him, she took an aggressive role, her tongue slipping between his lips. She greedily drew from him as much as she gave. His lower body responded in kind. Given their positions, she had to notice. Apparently she did. She wriggled off him and began unfastening his jeans with trembling hands.

Mike took a moment to study her. Her face was flushed and her lips glistened with moisture. His gaze slid lower. Her nipples puckered against the light flowered fabric. The evidence of her desire fueled his own.

"I never thought I'd agree to this again," she murmured.

"Oh, sweetheart, we're inevitable."

Her slender fingers shook as they grasped his zipper. That small involuntary movement hit him like a body blow. She was frantic, yes, but something more was involved. Something she'd been reluctant to admit.

He realized that he'd been more on target than he thought that afternoon. Like him, she too cared more than she wanted to. More than she was even conscious of.

He covered her fingers with his own, steadying the tremors in her hand. Together they made quick work of his jeans and briefs, sending them to a pile on the floor.

Mike didn't kid himself. His self-control had deserted him long ago. Only one thought occupied his mind—burying himself so deep inside her, he wouldn't know where he left off and she began. He lifted her dress and yanked the small scrap of lace down around her legs.

She gasped and Mike forced himself to stop. Their eyes met. If he'd frightened her, he'd pull back now. Somehow.

"I..." She hesitated.

"You what?" His words sounded more like a groan. If she wanted to stop, now was the time. A few seconds more and he doubted he'd be capable. "Say it."

She wrapped her arms around his neck. "I want you," she whispered. "Now."

After that there was no need for words. He rolled on his back, pulling her on top of him. Though he lacked the restraint necessary to move to a bed, he'd be damned if he'd bruise her soft body against the hard floor.

She raised herself upward and lifted her hips, lowering herself onto him in an excruciatingly drawn-out motion. The moment their bodies met, she uttered a soft moan. Her feminine noises coupled with her tempting heat had him gasping for breath.

She closed her eyes. He watched as myriad emotions shifted across her face. At that moment, he understood that he would never get enough of her, not ever.

* * *

With one smooth thrust, he entered her fully and filled her completely. Carly had never dreamed such a wash of emotions could accompany a physical act. Each time they came together was more explosive than the last.

She wondered if he felt it, too. She opened her eyes. As she gazed into the face she adored, she ran her fingers through his thick hair. In his golden eyes, she read every unspoken feeling she, herself, possessed. Words she'd never admit to aloud. He was right. She feared all they could have... feared having it and losing it at the same time.

This man reached inside her. He understood her without the need for words. He was her other half. And he would leave her soon. Because she loved him more than life itself, she would let him go. She pushed aside the doubt that assailed her, the niggling feeling that maybe they *could* work together toward a future.

Instead she draped herself across his chest, burying her face in the strong column of his neck. She wouldn't let him see her cry. His slight growth of beard scraped the skin on her face. Cheek to cheek, she nestled closer. He smelled of the ocean and of Mike. With a cough, she managed to choke back a sob.

He began to move beneath her. Each upward thrust was an expression of love, one she felt in every part of her body. She matched his motions until their surroundings faded and only they remained.

As he shuddered beneath her, she held him close. She kissed him as her own world erupted in a too brief but brilliant mixture of passion and love.

*   *   *

Carly's head rested on Mike's chest. Her hair tickled his nose and each breath he took was scented with vanilla.

"Let's go out for a late-night snack," Mike suggested.

"Don't you think we're a little underdressed?" Carly asked wryly.

He glanced down and grimaced. Her dress was hiked to mid-thigh and her bare legs were entwined with his. He was stark naked. For the first time he realized how little thought he had given to Carly. He hadn't bothered to undress her, let alone spared a moment to see if she'd been truly ready.

His only excuse was his driving need to block out her question. The time was fast approaching when he'd have to make a decision, whether his boss called or not. He couldn't keep running. Unmet obligations awaited him and the longer he stayed here, the longer he allowed himself the luxury of being with Carly, the harder it was to go back.

"Mike, that was a joke. What's wrong?" she asked, propping herself up on one elbow to look at him.

"Nothing." *Everything.* "Let's get out of here for a while. We've spent too much damn time in the house."

"Cabin fever already?" She drew herself to a sitting position and smoothed her skirt over her thighs.

"Not at all. But I thought you might like to go out. Like a real couple." A dangerous dream, he thought.

One that had but a slight chance of coming true.

"Oh. Sure." Her words were right, but they lacked feeling. She pushed her bangs off her forehead, a sure sign of trouble ahead.

He couldn't pinpoint the source of her anxiety, but he sensed it anyway.

"If we're going, I'd better shower." Bracing her hands against the floor, she started to rise.

"Hold it."

"What?"

"You tell me. One minute everything's fine and the next you've turned back into the old compliant Carly. What's bugging you?"

She turned, her normally expressive eyes blank. A haunted look shadowed her features. "Not a thing. Just tell me when you're ready to go," she said with patently false cheer and a forced smile.

Why did he suspect she was referring to a lot more than dinner?

TEN

Dinner was a strained event that Carly could have done without. Even the casual intimacy of the Mexican restaurant hadn't relaxed the tension. After her initial hesitation, she no longer doubted Mike's sincerity. She believed he genuinely wanted to spend an evening out rather than needing an escape from the restlessness she feared he'd begun to feel. But regardless of his reasons, she sensed their relationship inching toward its inevitable conclusion.

Though she understood Mike's inability to stick around, and though she'd expected it, waves of panic rippled through her anyway.

She clutched her water glass in an effort to stop the trembling in her hands. Thoughts of their earlier lovemaking did nothing to soothe her. Each of them had been frantic, as if they'd sensed that this time might be the last. For all she knew, it might have been.

"Dessert?" His deep voice intruded on her unpleasant thoughts. He held out a large plastic menu.

Like a peace offering, she accepted it and vowed to

appreciate whatever time they had left "After that vanilla shake you expect me to eat dessert?" She scanned the back page. "Fried ice cream sounds good," she said to the waiter, and licked her lips in anticipation.

Mike's burst of laughter broke the simmering tension that had surrounded them all evening. "I'm still hungry," she admitted sheepishly.

"Guess you worked up an appetite." His eyes gleamed with unchecked desire.

"Guess so." She swallowed hard. "Which means I'll just have to work it off later."

He treated her to a sexy grin. "You bet you will."

So she still had more time. How much? she wondered.

She felt like she was in possession of a time bomb, with the detonator ready to go off at any minute. Yes, she feared the moment in which he walked out of her life for good. But Mike was right. She also feared the consequences if they stayed together, feared he'd lose interest—or worse, that she would betray him. Although, looking at this man seated across from her, she doubted she'd ever be tempted to search elsewhere. What more could she possibly want?

So where did all her uncertainty leave her? she wondered. She glanced up. With a bowl of fried ice cream. The waiter cleared his throat and Carly moved her arm to make room for the luscious dessert. Caramel dripped over the sides. She cracked into the hard outer shell with a spoon, digging deep for the vanilla inside. Concentrating on her dish enabled her to escape reality and she took full advantage.

She placed the spoon between her lips, closed her eyes and savored the flavor. "Mmm."

* * *

Just like the cotton candy at Playland, Mike thought "Do you make eating food an erotic experience on purpose?" he asked. "Or does it just come naturally?"

A rosy blush colored her cheeks. "For a minute I forgot I wasn't alone." Clearly embarrassed, she pushed the plate toward the center of the table.

He nudged it back. "Don't mind me, I enjoy watching." He adored her feminine curves and ability to enjoy life without censoring it, calories included.

She shrugged and dug the spoon back into the caramel for another bite.

"How's the column coming?"

"Not bad. I finished next month's questions and answers and faxed them over to the magazine."

"What about the book?"

"Format's done." She paused for a sip of water. "Three distinct segments should work."

"What are the topics?" He leaned back in his chair

and eyed her intently.

"You're really interested?"

"Of course. Why wouldn't I be?"

She bit down on her lower lip. "You could be just being polite."

Beneath the table, he clenched his hands into tight fists. "I don't do polite. Not for the hell of it anyway."

She nodded. Blonde strands of hair fell free from her loose braid and framed her face before she tucked them behind one ear. "I knew that."

Did she? He silently cursed his brother's reappearance since it had obviously brought back insecurities he thought she had let go. "But maybe I was just humoring you."

"Were you?"

This time he cursed aloud. "Let's get something straight. I don't humor any more than I do polite. It's condescending to us both."

Her gaze dropped to her plate. The ice cream, he noticed, had begun to melt. "If I wasn't interested, I wouldn't have asked," he said in a harsh voice meant to capture her attention.

It did. Her eyelids fluttered upward, and startled, her gaze met his. "Fine," she said in just as clipped a tone as he'd used on her.

At least she was on the offensive, he thought. "And while we're at it, I'd appreciate it if you'd remember one thing: I'm not Peter. I don't act like him and I sure as hell don't think like him." His hand came down hard on the table, causing the water in both their glasses to slosh over the top.

She grinned. "Personally, I agree with you. And believe it or not, I appreciate the reminder."

He let out a deep breath. The strain of this meal had begun to wear on him. Every possible emotion had passed between them and he was exhausted. He signaled for the check.

"Just one more bite." Taking advantage of her last spoonful, Mike watched as she licked the utensil clean, running her tongue over the sticky caramel coating to remove every remaining bit.

Desire hit him hard. His exhaustion disappeared in the wake of physical need. As he shamelessly followed every movement, he wondered if he was destined to be in her spell forever. Every damn thing she made him feel was good. Even when there was trouble hovering between them, she made him feel alive. But so did taking pictures and capturing the world on film. At least it always had before. Why was the thought so much less appealing now? Mike sensed the answer had less to do with the painful episode in the Middle East and more to do with Carly.

Get out, he thought.

While he still could.

He forced his gaze upward. Her beautiful brown eyes shimmered with amusement. "Want some?" she asked and dipped the spoon back into the half-melted ice cream.

He opened his mouth to answer and she hand-fed him the dessert. He wasn't sure if the sweetness came from the gooey dish or the woman who gave it to him. "Incredible," he said. His gaze locked with hers.

Reaching over, she wiped what must have been a trace of ice cream or caramel from his bottom lip. Her gentle touch finished him off.

He tossed his napkin down onto the table. "Let's go." With a glance at the check the waiter had placed on the edge of the table, he shoved his hand into his pocket and retrieved his wallet. He peeled off the bills and tossed them down.

The moment he stood, he was grateful for the dark lighting. His jeans were way too tight. Grasping her hand, he tugged and led her out of the restaurant and into the dark night.

The car was parked behind the restaurant, and thanks to the late hour that area of the parking lot had all but emptied out. Mike didn't know how it happened. One minute he'd been leading her toward the car, the next he'd bracketed her body between the himself and the metal door.

*   *   *

Carly gazed up at him, hope and expectancy warring in her heart. She'd been sending out mixed signals all evening, she knew. But she wasn't mixed up anymore. She wanted him for the time they had left. She licked at her dry lips.

And he wanted her. The hard erection pressed against her told her that.

He reached out and traced her moist lower lip with the pad of his finger. With his gaze never leaving hers, he placed his finger in his own mouth. "Sweet," he whispered.

"It's the caramel." She gripped his waist with both hands. He was her anchor in so many different ways.

"No," he said, shaking his head, "it's you. You always taste sweet to me."

A strange sensation gripped her chest. More emotional than physical, tears threatened to fall but she pushed them back. "You don't do polite and you don't humor me, but I do think you're just saying that so you can get lucky."

"Did it work?" Something about the hesitancy in his voice spoke to her. They'd been dancing around each other all night and for what? They understood each other too well, knew each other's deepest fears.

They knew the end was coming.

"It would have worked without the sweet talk," she murmured, grasping his face in both hands.

The kiss that came next was anything but sweet; in fact, *hot* was the only word that came to Carly's mind before she became so engulfed with Mike that she didn't want to think at all. She locked her leg around his ankle, securing him against her. The ridge of his arousal was firm and hard against her stomach and his warm breath fanned her neck as he trailed wet, seductive kisses down her collarbone. Cool air drifted over her damp skin, increasing the power of her desire.

He dipped the strap of her dress down over one shoulder and edged a fingertip above the swell of her breast. She exhaled, but a slow moan escaped instead. She anticipated his hot mouth on her breast, wanted his heated touch more than she wanted her next breath. And if the glazed but intense look in his eyes was any indication, she'd have it too. Carly closed her eyes, waiting, wanting…

A car horn honked and loud laughter sounded behind them. "Go for it, man." A group of rowdy teenagers waved and gunned the engine, leaving dust in their wake.

"You sure you want to keep giving kids like that a helping hand?" Mike muttered. He leaned his head against hers, his breathing coming in harsh, labored gasps.

Carly wanted to be mortified, but she couldn't suppress a laugh instead. "It's either that or let them out on their own…"

He shook his head. "Carly…" His husky voice held promise.

The dead silence of the night surrounded them. Her pulse beat faster as she answered his unspoken question by placing her hand inside his. "Let's go home."

Minutes later they entered the house. By unspoken agreement, she followed him toward his room. Something made her stop in the family room and pick up the house phone. She heard the beep, beep, beep that indicated that there was a voicemail. Carly dialed the code and put the phone on speaker.

She didn't recognize the voice. She knew she wouldn't. Yet as soon as the deep baritone sounded in the empty room, she wished she could press delete or turn back the clock and not even have stopped to check the voicemail. Somehow, she knew.

And when Mike's hand went to his bad shoulder, her fears were confirmed. Pain sliced through her as the message wound its way to completion. "Relaxation time's over. We could use you on assignment. Same place, different setup. Pack your bags and get the first flight out, buddy. It's time to move on."

*　　*　　*

Carly stood behind him. Bracing himself, Mike turned

to face her. Moonlight filtered in through an open window, illuminating an otherwise dark room. Her eyes had taken on the bleak, haunted look he had seen earlier. To her credit, though, her shoulders were squared as she tried to look unaffected. Too bad he wasn't buying the act.

The time had come sooner than he had planned. Leaving her would be next to impossible, but he had no choice. He wondered if she would beg him to stay. Part of him longed for that security while another dreaded the confrontation.

He almost laughed aloud. For a moment he had forgotten her feelings about their relationship. She might just welcome his departure. His entire body turned cold at the thought.

"Mike?" she asked in an unsteady voice.

"What?"

"I have one favor to ask."

"Okay, but I can't promise anything." No matter how much he wanted to.

"This you can."

"What is it?"

Tears shimmered in her dark eyes. "Don't wake me to say good-bye."

She should have begged him to stay. That and a body blow would have been less painful than the plaintive but resigned note in Carly's voice. She was going to let him go. Mike thought he had been prepared.

He had been wrong. "Sit down." Pausing to flick on a lamp, he prodded her toward the living room couch.

He dropped onto the soft cushion and patted the empty space next to him. She sat. But her silence unnerved him more than any hysterical scene.

"Tell me about the sections of your book," he said.

"What?" Startled, she looked up at him.

He cupped her chin in his hand and stared into her eyes. "We have tonight."

"And you want to spend it talking about my book?" She blinked and a lone teardrop leaked down her cheek. He caught it with his thumb, pausing to lick the salt off his finger.

"I want to spend it with you. In case you don't realize it, sex isn't the only thing between us." He couldn't leave letting her believe he cared only for the good time they'd had in bed. Given her inherent fear, the possibility shook him to the core. So he would spend what little time they had left condensing a few more weeks of intimate discussion into one night.

He drew a deep breath. "I care about you. All of you."

"You do?"

He slanted her a look meant to chastise.

"Sorry," she murmured.

"You should be." He let his hand come to rest on her shoulder. "Why do you keep doubting me?"

She flicked her bangs out of her eyes. A gesture that had become second nature to her and so familiar to Mike that it caused a warmth in the region of his heart… because she used it whenever he touched hers.

"I can't remember the last person who cared enough about me to ask something so… trivial."

"Since when is your career trivial?"

She shook her head. "To me it's not. But to other people…" Her shoulders lifted and fell.

"Hey."

Raising her long lashes, she looked at him with wide eyes.

"Don't I deserve a label a little more personal than *other people*?"

"Yeah, I guess you do." She laughed, a light-hearted sound that, despite the tense and somber circumstances, sounded natural, not forced. A sound Mike knew he would carry with him wherever he went.

"Progress." Releasing an exaggerated groan, he propped his feet up on the couch, prompting her to shift and join him laying down or be dislodged.

"So. How do you go about solving the problems of the American teenager?"

Carly leaned her head against his chest and snuggled closer so she wouldn't topple onto the floor. Enjoying his warmth and needing his strength had nothing to do with her actions. "Name your biggest problem as a teen," she said.

"Family," he said without hesitation.

Thinking about his parents' deaths and his disinterested aunt and uncle, she could only imagine the depth of the dysfunction he'd lived. "And after family?" she asked.

"Sex."

She nudged him in the side with her elbow.

He groaned. "Direct hit," he muttered. "I meant girls."

"Relationships," she clarified. "And from a teenage girls' perspective, it was probably friends and then relationships," she said in a purely authoritative tone.

"I like this take-charge side of you," he said, wrapping his arms around her waist and resting his chin on her shoulder.

She laughed. "Normally I handle myself pretty well. You just came into my life at… a crossroads."

"You'll get through it. I have faith. So tell me, how far have you gotten on each section?" he asked, then listened intently as she filled him in on her progress— or lack thereof.

His interest warmed her. He obviously cared for her, for more than just the physical relationship they'd shared. And despite his imminent departure, he'd proven the kind of man he really was. The kind who wouldn't be content to leave friends and responsibilities hanging. The kind who would face his fears and move on, leaving her behind.

She snuggled closer into his embrace. Letting him go would be harder than she had thought, but he'd never expressed an interest in anything long-term, never even indicated he'd want to stay. She ignored the little voice reminding her that she hadn't exactly encouraged him, either.

Lacing his fingers through hers, he rested their hands together on her stomach. "I know you'll finish that book and make me proud."

He laughed, and the deep rumble passed right through her. "If I can get past my own family history, maybe."

"I have faith, but we'll see, won't we?"

No, we won't. Because he wouldn't be around. "Will you be okay?" she asked, hating her unsteady voice and the trembling in her body.

"I'll be fine. I promise." He pressed a gentle kiss against her cheek.

Carly closed her eyes, fighting the tears his touch inspired. She knew his promise wasn't within his power to keep, but she let the words lie. She needed to hear them, to keep them close to her heart.

"You can handle this, Mike." Bolstering his confidence, even when her own was flagging, was the least she could do for the man she loved. And she did love him. No sense in denying the truth to herself. Not now. "And once you go back, you'll understand that. Everything you love is waiting for you."

"Not everything." His arms grasped her tighter, making it difficult to draw a breath.

She didn't care. For tonight, his embrace was the only thing that mattered.

They lay in silence. The clock in the hallway mocked them as it loudly ticked away the moments of the night. With each passing minute, dawn came closer.

Carly didn't realize she had dozed off. When she awoke, she had a stiff neck from her position on the couch. She knew without looking around.

Mike was gone.

He had kept his promise. He hadn't woken her to say good-bye.

And they hadn't made love, either.

*   *   *

For the next month, Carly indulged her need to mourn a relationship that was over before it had begun. She hadn't mourned the loss of her fiancé, but Mike's departure affected her in a much more profound way.

He wasn't just a man who'd passed through her life. He'd touched her life and made it better. He'd made *her* better.

She found it difficult to touch food; even yogurt and liquid wouldn't pass the lump in her throat. She puttered around the bright kitchen and attempted to block out the memories of love, laughter and lobsters, without any success. So she turned her attention to her work, finding not solace but refuge from the painful truths that surrounded her.

But she couldn't hide out forever. When she couldn't stand the bright sunshine beating down on the beach since her own mood was so gray, she decided the time had come for change. Self-absorption and wallowing in pity wouldn't solve anything. Like Mike, she needed to reclaim her life. As fast as she had packed up and traveled to the Hamptons, she re-packed and headed for the city.

Once back in familiar surroundings, she pulled herself together. She contacted the school and put herself on call for students who needed summer counseling. She worked on both her book and some new column ideas until she was so exhausted that she fell into bed each night both mentally and physically drained. She met Juliette for dinner and drinks, some of her friends for lunch, and tried to resume her life.

But she still dreamed of Mike. His laugh, his sexy

swagger, his lips on hers. Nothing distracted her and nothing came easily. Not even the book. Looking back on all the work she'd done over the summer, she found length but not depth. Oh, the friendship section had fared well enough, but not the relationship or family portions. She hadn't expected them to be simple. But carrying Mike's faith deep inside her heart, she'd managed to put together a rough draft of both. Though she wanted to be pleased, she couldn't because the effort lacked heart. Perhaps because her own was so badly damaged.

With Mike gone and too many hours to fill, soul-searching became her favorite pastime. She needed to heal. Until she dealt with her irrational fears, she would never be free to commit to anyone or anything else. She couldn't change how things had ended with Mike. She hadn't asked him to stay because she knew how badly he'd needed to face his past, and how much he loved his career.

And because she hadn't had the guts.

Despite the fact that she'd turned off the air-conditioner in her apartment, she shivered and wrapped herself in a blanket to ward off the chill. She rose and headed for the kitchen. A hot cup of tea would warm her inside and out. After fumbling around, she resettled herself on the couch.

The teddy bear Mike had won in Playland stared at

her with large, accusing eyes. The beautiful memories paraded through her mind and settled in her heart.

So did the guilt. She'd allowed Mike to enter a dangerous situation without telling him the truth. She loved him. Whether or not she was capable of committing to that love, regardless of the fact that he *hadn't* been, he'd deserved to know.

What if something terrible happened again, only this time he didn't make it? Then he would never know someone in his life truly loved him.

Loved him and essentially abandoned him, just as he believed his parents had. Laying her head in her hands, Carly wept. For Mike and for herself.

* * *

There was no way she would let her past control her future. Carly drew a deep breath and followed her father into his study. The decision to come here hadn't been easy, but it had been inevitable. She couldn't find herself as a person or have a life if she was still mired in her adolescent pain.

She knew, without asking, that she and her father would have the opportunity to talk in private. Her mother hadn't missed a weekly card game in fifteen years. Carly glanced around at the rich mahogany bookshelves her father had had installed when he'd moved out of the city to Westchester County. Though he still kept his apartment in Manhattan, it was more a place for weekend stays and work emergencies than his home.

She glanced around. Nothing in this room had changed since she was a teenager. Nothing and everything, just like her life. She clenched her fists. Her father stood across the room, obviously waiting for her to speak. When it became clear she didn't know where to start, he cleared his throat "I was surprised when you called and *asked* if you could come. Most daughters don't need permission to visit their fathers."

She turned to face him. "I'm not most daughters... and you're not most fathers."

"No, I'm not." His easy agreement surprised her, and she studied him more closely. His light hair was now more silver than tawny in color, and the dark circles beneath his eyes were a bit more prominent. But overall he looked well.

She couldn't have this conversation standing up, so she gestured toward the couch and chairs in the center of the room. She chose her favorite seat as a child, an oversized, beat-up leather club chair and ottoman. Her father sat on the matching chair beside her.

"So..." She curled her feet beneath her.

"So. If you're here, there's a reason. What can I do to make it better?" he asked.

"What do you mean?"

"I'm assuming you need something. Or someone to talk to, and picked me."

"Why would you think that?" Her relationship with Mike, such as it was, and her fear of passion and commitment weren't things she'd expect her father to be aware of. Funny how she'd accused Mike of being incapable of commitment when she suffered from the same thing herself. She just hadn't known it at the time. Commitment to Peter wasn't the same as commitment to someone she loved with her whole heart and soul. That frightened her to death.

Roger cleared his throat. "We had a company cocktail party a few nights ago. Peter mentioned that his brother was back overseas."

Carly tensed. "So?"

"So, I met with Mike. He's nothing like his brother."

She smiled. "I know."

"Judging by that glowing look on your face, I'd say that's a good thing. You can't be happy he's gone."

"And you think I'm here to talk about my love life?"

He shifted uncomfortably in his seat and a sheepish look crossed his face. "When you called, I didn't know what to think. But I knew if I didn't push, we wouldn't make any progress. I'm sorry if I'm prying." Apparently, after all this time, father-daughter talks didn't come easy for him either.

She sighed. "You're not. I'm here, so we might as well say what's on our minds."

"Well, Pete seems to think you sent Mike away because of the pain he had caused you. He tends to ramble on when he has my ear, but I wondered."

Laughter bubbled inside her, breaking some of her inner tension. Startled, her father's shocked gaze met hers. "Who else but Peter would think so highly of himself?" she asked. "As if my whole life was affected by what *he* did."

Her father chuckled but sobered fast. "I know better than to think that. Your whole life was affected by what *I* did. And I wish it was ego talking, but it isn't."

Leave it to her father, the straight-talking attorney, to force the issue and conversation to the real reason she'd come. "Well, knowing Peter, he probably believes I lost endless nights of sleep mourning him."

Roger smiled back at her. "In his favor, I think he was trying to make amends between us by feeding me information I could use to approach you."

"Always look for an ulterior motive," she cautioned, still smiling. To her surprise, she and Roger were sharing an honest father-daughter moment. A rarity in her life. "I'll bet he even thinks I turned to Mike on the rebound."

"You didn't." More statement than question, Roger looked Carly in the eye.

"No," she whispered. But she'd turned him away, and her father's indiscretion had been the catalyst. She'd been afraid to commit to Mike. Not because she feared repeating Roger's affair, but because, as Mike had once said, she was afraid of repeating Roger's mistakes in his marriage.

So she'd come to face her father's past in order to move forward with her present. "Why didn't you? Approach me, I mean? When Peter gave you all that information, why didn't you come talk to me?"

He had the grace to look ashamed. "Because I knew you would turn me away. At least I feared you would."

Her hand rested on the armrest of the brown leather chair, and her father covered her hand with his own. The comforting touch soothed her, making her wonder why she'd waited so long to come to the one man she'd needed so badly in her life.

That was one mistake she didn't want to repeat again with Mike... if he ever returned to the States.

"He was much more than a rebound, wasn't he?" Roger asked quietly.

"He was. I mean, he is."

"So what are you going to do about it?"

Carly bit back a sigh. It was one thing to talk about

their family, another to discuss her relationship with Mike. It felt awkward and uncomfortable, but she should have known her father would be persistent. He was a trial lawyer, after all.

"You know, this all strikes me as hypocritical. You weren't willing to talk when I needed you. Why should I open up to you now?"

"Because after all these years, you came to me. And because after all these years, you deserve an explanation. Whether your mother approves or not."

"I'm not sure if I do or not, but it needs to be said," Anne said as she walked into the room. The three of them faced each other—three individuals who hadn't been a family for so long.

Anne's early return caught Carly by surprise, and she glanced at her father's guilty face. He'd called her mother home for this meeting. Well, better all at once than one at a time, she supposed. Still, her stomach churned in nervous anticipation.

Anne sat on the couch and Roger joined her, clasping her hand in his. Carly narrowed her eyes, seeing reality as if for the first time. Had her parents done more than made peace with their lives? Had they truly come together after all this time? Carly shook her head. They'd obviously done more than made peace, but it hadn't happened overnight. She'd just closed them out of her life and shut her eyes to the progress they'd made in the years following the scandal and her lonely childhood.

Carly sat alone. She faced her parents, who now sat together on the sofa, united in a way she hadn't understood until now.

"We didn't talk about things because *I* insisted. I thought if we just put it behind us, it would go away." Anne fiddled with a ring on her hand, twisting it in a nervous gesture.

"If you don't acknowledge things, they can't hurt you," Carly murmured in repetition of the phrase her mother had ingrained in her over the years. Only now did Carly realize that that philosophy had taught her to avoid personal confrontation and dealing with reality.

"And I went along," her father continued. "I'd promised. The only way your mother would take me back was to pretend it never happened. After all I'd put her though, that one request wasn't too much to ask." He met Carly's gaze. "I see now I was wrong. *We* were wrong. In saving our marriage, we made you the victim."

His words were so on target that a lump rose in Carly's throat and remained there.

"But not on purpose." Anne came up beside Carly and knelt down beside her. "I thought I was protecting you. Honest to goodness, I believed I was doing the right thing for us all."

Carly blinked back tears. "I know you did." Although nothing could change the past, at least they were talking now. "But I have to know something."

Anne swallowed hard. "Anything," she said, and Carly understood for the first time how difficult that word was for her mother to say.

"Did you love each other once?" she asked in a small voice that sounded so childlike, it was pitiful. But she knew for certain she'd walk out of this room a much stronger person than she had been coming in.

"I have always loved your father," Anne said slowly. "And he has always loved me."

Carly cleared her throat and turned to her father. "Then... why?" Why have an affair? Why go looking outside his marriage for something they'd started out with from the beginning?

Her father nodded, seeming to understand without hearing the rest of the words. "I can answer that."

"No, I will." Anne began, "Because I didn't know how to show that love and I drove him away with silence and lack of communication."

"But I shouldn't have strayed. I should have tried harder to make things work. Spent more time at home and less time focusing on my career. It shouldn't have taken an affair and a tragedy to set us on the right course."

They each accepted blame. They'd each come to

terms with their lives. It seemed only Carly continued to live in past shadows. "And you are? On the right course, I mean?" Carly asked.

Her mother had reseated herself on the couch and her father grabbed for Anne's hand. "We've been in counseling for years. Each time we tried to make an overture, you turned us away. We didn't blame you, but we couldn't figure out a way to make things right for you either."

Carly smiled. "Because it wasn't your job. I'm a grown-up, and I chose to be ruled by the past." But not anymore.

"We're so sorry. *I'm* so sorry."

She shook her head, then wiped the tears that dripped down her face. "You know, we're all to blame in a way. But..."

"I want to start over," Anne said. "I know it's too late to be the mother you should have had, but I want more than we've had lately. It's selfish, but..."

Carly didn't wait for her to finish. Without thinking, she joined her parents on the couch... and became part of her family once more.

ELEVEN

"Hi. I'd like to cancel my subscription to your paper." Carly spoke to the faceless telephone operator.

"You can't shut your eyes, Carly." Juliette kicked her feet out onto the cocktail table across from the couch. "It's on television and the radio, too. Do you have the name of his boss? Or maybe Peter has news…"

Ignoring her friend, Carly repeated the newspaper operator's question aloud. "Why cancel?" Because she hadn't been able to face her morning coffee and the news of the day without reading about the war torn country where Mike had gone. The news was never good and the result was too many nightmares and not enough sleep.

She sighed. "My schedule just doesn't work and I haven't been reading. I'm sorry." She juggled the phone. "No, I don't even want tomorrow's paper. Thanks." She hung up and stared at the months' worth of papers on the table.

"The recycling dump is going to love you," Juliette said.

Since Carly had forgotten to cancel her subscription before leaving for the summer, her considerate neighbor had taken in her back copies of the *Times* while she was away, keeping them for her return. Stacks of papers would have blatantly advertised an apartment ripe for theft, and Carly was grateful that a friend had been aware. She hadn't thought beyond getting away.

And she hadn't known what awaited her once she got back.

She lifted the top paper and the headlines jumped out at her, taking on a life of their own. Another small, war-torn country. More injured... She tossed the paper aside. She closed her eyes but couldn't escape the harrowing visions that plagued her.

Juliette draped a soft arm around her shoulders and gave Carly a friendly squeeze. "These aren't helping." She scooped up the remainder of the newspapers and headed for the disposal in the hall.

"You're a good friend," Carly said when the older woman returned.

"So are you. Now, what do you say we go for a walk? Clear your head and maybe you can figure out a way to contact that man and..."

"No!"

"Why not? You love him; you've admitted as much."

"Because how *I* feel isn't what matters. He left, Jules. I didn't ask him to stay, but it doesn't matter. If he wanted to be in the States, he'd be here regardless of me. I have no right to interfere in a life he loves. He isn't one for commitment. I always knew that."

This wasn't a case of accepting and avoiding, it was one of understanding the man she loved and moving on. A loud rapping sound caused her to jump. She rubbed her damp hands on her jeans and headed for the door. She peered through the peephole and her stomach did an involuntary flip.

She hadn't seen Peter since the Hamptons. His appearance now couldn't be good news. Carly flung the door open wide. "What's wrong?" she asked before she said hello. "Is he…"

"He's alive," he said in a reassuring voice. He placed a hand on her arm. "But…"

She glanced at his drawn face. He didn't look as if he'd had much sleep the night before. "He's alive *but?* What is it? You're scaring me."

She grabbed his wrist and pulled him into the apartment. She felt Juliette's hand on her shoulder for support and her heart swelled inside her chest. "Out with it Peter."

He let out a deep breath. "Mike's back, but he's in

the hospital."

*   *   *

The next hour passed in a foggy haze. Carly barely recalled the taxi ride to the hospital. Only the fact that Juliette had begged her to call with news and Peter had shoved her into the backseat registered in her memory.

She ran down a long corridor and stopped short before the door indicated by the hall nurse. "You go on. You're his brother."

"Now's not the time to argue over who's more important," Peter said and gave her a nudge in the ribs.

"Ouch." She shot him a dirty look. "Watch it before you do some permanent damage."

"Quit stalling." He drew his arm back as if to give her a second push.

"Okay," she muttered, mentally acknowledging that fear held her back. She let out a deep breath and opened the door.

The room was small and antiseptic in appearance as well as smell. Beige walls and white bedsheets did little to add cheer to an otherwise bland atmosphere. Her heart thudded against her ribs and she glanced toward the bed where Mike lay, apparently asleep.

Quietly, so as not to disturb him, she tiptoed into the room and pulled out the chair next to the bed. She sat, then lifted his warm hand and clutched it between her own. Love rose deep within her and filled the emptiness that his departure had created. The need to throw herself into his arms and stay there forever grew with each passing second.

The panic that used to automatically follow her intense feelings for Mike didn't surface this time because, thanks to her parents, she'd learned a lot. Like the fact that the father she'd accused of not honoring his commitments had done just that. By returning to his marriage and making it work, he wasn't the man of disgrace she'd believed, but a man of conscience.

Like Mike. Another man she'd accused of not knowing the first thing about keeping promises. His return abroad was proof... She'd been wrong again.

She let her gaze rake over him, and she took in the fact that he was home and safe. Carly gave a silent prayer of thanks that he would be okay. It wasn't nearly enough. Peter had reassured her many times on the ride over that Mike wasn't injured, merely out of commission. Never before had her ex-fiancé's words given her so much comfort.

Mike stirred in his sleep and her gaze focused again on his face. Though he had only been gone a month, his hair was noticeably longer. He hadn't shaved at all during his stint abroad and his almost full beard did little to dim his sexy good looks. Despite the gray pallor beneath the tanned skin, he possessed that *give 'em hell* look she'd come to associate with Mike.

With care, she pushed a stray lock of hair off his forehead. When his golden eyes opened, relief washed through her and she smiled. "You're the only man I know who can spend a month in a war-torn country and come home unharmed only to get blindsided by appendicitis."

He grinned, but she could see the gesture took a great deal of effort. "You always knew I was unique." He motioned toward the plastic water jug.

She poured for him and he gulped the entire cup. "Better?" she asked.

"Much."

Silence filled the small room. Carly glanced over her shoulder and realized that Peter had sent her in alone. She turned back to Mike. "I was worried," she said in a whisper.

"I wanted to come back sooner."

"You did what you needed to. I understood that." She fingered her bangs. The desire to admit her feelings was overwhelming, but his weakened state stopped her. So did the fact that she had no idea how he felt in return.

Yes, he was back, but for how long this time, she wondered. And even if he was to stay, what kind of future could they have? What was she capable of giving to him, and he to her?

"Can I get you anything else?" she asked instead.

He shook his head.

"Now that I know you're okay, Peter's waiting in the hall." She rose, carefully releasing her grip on his hand. Before she could take a step, he caught her arm in a surprisingly strong grip for a man just out of surgery.

"Wait."

Carly swallowed hard and tried to keep her inner panic from showing on her face. Deep, cleansing breaths, she silently ordered. When dizziness assaulted her, she knew she'd been unsuccessful.

"I'm not running anymore," he said, in a voice still rough from medication but also tight with emotion.

"I know. You're flat on your back," she quipped with more lightness than she felt.

"You can't joke your way out of this. We need to talk."

"And you need to rest."

Mike closed his eyes. Apparently she was right. The exhaustion was evident on his face and every forced word he spoke.

"You're right," he said finally.

"I usually am." She smiled.

"Am I interrupting?" His brother pushed open the

door to the hospital room.

Mike leaned his head back against the stack of hospital pillows and groaned. "Come on in," Carly called out, saving him the effort. She turned to Peter. "I was just leaving." She squeezed Mike's hand once and headed for the door without meeting his gaze.

*   *   *

Mike leaned back against the uncomfortable pillow and waited while Carly slipped out the door. A floor nurse walked in behind Peter. "Hey, Pete."

His brother grinned. "Looking better. I have to admit you scared the living daylights out of me."

"Doubling over in the airport wasn't my idea of a good time either." He waited while the nurse did her thing—temperature and blood pressure.

"All set, Mr. Novack." She jotted notes in his chart and walked out.

"If I had known about those good-looking nurses, I would have checked myself in here," Pete said, his eyes following the attractive nurse's departure.

"You're one of a kind, little brother." Mike eased himself higher in the bed, ignoring the pain as well as the painkiller the nurse had tried to force on him. He preferred having a clear head.

"I am, aren't I?" Pete chuckled. "When are they releasing you?"

"Not soon enough," Mike muttered.

"What's your hurry?" His brother glanced back toward the closed door, but no voluptuous blonde nurse answered his silent plea.

Mike laughed, then clenched his teeth at the accompanying pain in his side. "I can't get my life together from a hospital bed."

Carly had visited him twice yesterday and once already today. Each time she had stayed longer but left as soon as the questions turned personal.

"She's playing hard to get?" Pete asked.

"She just needs some coaxing," Mike said, deliberately vague. He had no intention of discussing his relationship, or lack thereof, with Pete.

His brother paced the room. "I know she's worth the effort," he said at last.

"Having second thoughts?"

"Hell no." Pete laughed. "She's all yours. Carly and I wouldn't make each other happy," he said.

Mike raised his eyebrows in surprise. "Since when does happiness count?" he asked his work-devoted brother.

Pete sat himself on the chair next to Mike's bed. "Since I nearly destroyed someone who was nothing but good to me. And since Regina expected to marry the newest litigation partner on her way up the corporate ladder."

"Didn't like being on the other end of things, huh? There might be hope for you yet, little brother."

"Don't get carried away," Pete muttered.

Mike laughed. "Well, you did good letting Carly know after the hospital notified you."

He shrugged uncomfortably. "It was the least I could do. You're my brother, after all."

Mike nodded. It was something Carly had reminded him of time and again. He needed his brother, something he wouldn't have been able to admit prior to his return to the Middle East. He could face that truth now.

Along with many others. He only hoped it wasn't too late.

*   *   *

Carly stepped out of the bathroom to the sound of an insistent ring. "I'm coming," she called to her impatient visitor. She'd just gotten out of the shower and finished blow-drying her hair, probably missing the first couple of rings. Whoever was out there had his finger permanently attached to her doorbell. She opened the door a crack and glanced beyond the chain lock.

"Mike?" She closed the door to unlatch the lock. "What are you doing here?" He wasn't due to be released from the hospital until the next day.

"I couldn't take that place another minute." He smiled and headed straight for *his* chair. Holding his right side, he lowered himself slowly and dropped a duffel bag onto the floor. "I'll never take being mobile for granted again."

Carly stopped in the kitchen for a glass of ice water and tried to calm the pounding of her heart. She wasn't ready for this conversation, not without warning. Apparently, though, Mike had set the timetable. She'd just have to listen… and hope he hadn't come to tell her he was leaving again as soon as he was able.

"You checked out against doctor's orders, I'll bet." She handed him the glass and sat down on the couch.

He shrugged. "Another day or night wasn't going to make a difference."

"I'm sure your doctor had other ideas." She chewed on her lower lip. Finally, curiosity got the better of her. "Where are you staying?" Until he was healed, she didn't have to worry about him hopping on the nearest airplane out of the country. At least not yet. She fingered her bangs. Her hand trembled and she shoved it beneath her leg.

"I'll stay with Pete for a week or so." Mike deliberately paused for a sip of water and watched her reaction.

She nodded slowly. "And then?" Her lips, which

had been damp before, had lost their luster as she nibbled on her lower lip with her teeth.

*   *   *

"What do you expect me to do?"

Startled, she met his gaze. Her brown eyes reflected confusion and something else. What, he didn't know. Since his return, he hadn't been able to read her as easily as before.

"Do you expect me to head overseas?"

"I… I don't know what to expect."

He placed his glass down, rose carefully and resettled himself next to her on the couch. "There was a time when I didn't either."

"And now you do?"

He nodded. "You accused me of not understanding the concept of commitment once, and as much as that hurt, it was the truth."

She shook her head. "I was wrong. You've always been committed to your job, to your brother. To me, when you set your mind to proving certain points," she said with a grin.

He placed his hand beneath her chin, turning her so their eyes locked. "Committed to running away. It's not the same thing."

"Maybe not," she murmured.

"Definitely not. Until you damn near married my

brother, I didn't realize what a mess I'd made of my life. That was a wake-up call if I'd ever gotten one."

"I thought you provided *me* with the wake-up call." She smiled, the gesture so warm and open, he nearly forgot the last month of deprivation.

"We're good for each other." If her appearance was any indication, she'd missed him as much as he'd ached for her. She'd lost weight in the time they'd been apart. Slender legs were encased in tight leggings and suede boots. Her freshly blow-dried hair trailed over an oversized white sweater that hugged her thighs. And shadows lurked in her dark eyes. Shadows he'd do his damndest to remove, if she'd let him.

He touched her soft cheek with one knuckle. "In your own quiet way, you showed me all I was missing.

She shook her head. "I abandoned you." She didn't meet his gaze.

"No." Pulling her against him, he buried his face in her hair and inhaled the scent he'd only had the luxury of dreaming of. "You cared enough to let me go when I needed to."

In a move that stunned him, she jerked backward, removing herself from his arms and distancing herself from his touch. She stood. Tears ran unchecked down her cheeks.

"Don't give me so much credit." She shook her head and laughed, a harsh sound that tore at his heart.

"I let you go because it was easier than walking away myself. But if you hadn't gotten that call, don't think for a minute I wouldn't have found an excuse to pull away."

He stood and remained silent. Nothing she said came as a shock to him, nor did it bother him the way she obviously thought it should. "And?"

"Don't you get it? I wanted you to go." She obviously felt she owed him the truth.

He respected her for that, he thought, watching her sink back into the couch. "And you wanted me to come back, just as much as I wanted to come back to you." He stayed silent until she looked at him. "I went because I had to and came back for the same reasons."

"I don't understand."

Or she didn't want to. The glimmer Mike saw in her eyes wasn't happiness, it was uncertainty, and his heart clenched with the same emotion. Because, for the first time, he acknowledged that he might actually lose her.

"Commitment," he explained. "I had to complete one before I could make another." He leaned over. Lowering his head to hers, he tasted her lips, reveling in the sweetness that was uniquely Carly. His mouth moved over hers, coaxing and teasing, seeking acceptance. Her resistance fled in seconds, with a soft sigh and an intimate greeting. Her tongue met his and

Mike's self-control went into remaining gentle but insistent. He couldn't, wouldn't lose her now.

She raked her fingers through his hair as she allowed him to draw her closer. He brushed feather-light kisses on the tip of her nose and across her jaw. He sat beside her and drew her close. She didn't pull away and that gave him hope.

Now he owed her honesty. "Orphaned isn't abandoned. Do you remember telling me that?" He separated them so he could look into her brown eyes.

She nodded.

"I didn't understand then. Until I spent time with those kids from the accident, I couldn't. But I realize, now, that I was still feeling like a lost kid... and pushing away any chance of ever settling down. Running from one job to the next without any long-term commitment, not letting anyone close to me... because I didn't want to give anyone the chance to leave me again."

"Including me?"

"Especially you. Because you meant more to me than anyone else. So I left you first."

She shook her head and laughed, but it wasn't a pleasant sound. "Some pair we are."

"But I came back. The appendicitis hit once I'd already landed, but I came back. Do you understand now?" he asked.

She pressed a kiss to his neck but remained silent causing his heart to thud painfully against his chest. Mike grasped her arms in front of her, holding her before him, begging her to listen and understand. "We both had things to deal with, things to face. There's no shame in that."

"I know. I wasn't any better at dealing with the past than you were. But that's changed. While you were gone, I made peace with my parents."

Pride swelled inside him and her words gave him hope. "I know what that took for you."

She nodded. "And I learned something."

"What was that?"

"That my perception of safety was as false as my perception of life. *Nothing* about Peter was safe."

Mike reached for the duffel bag he'd dropped earlier and pulled out a stack of photos. "Look."

Carly accepted the pile and flipped through the pictures. "Rye Playland," she said, feeling the smile on her lips.

"Take a look at yourself."

She did and was surprised by what she saw. Wide smiles, huge laughing eyes... and they were hers. "I was happy," she whispered.

"*We* were happy."

"What are you saying?"

"Just what I said in the hospital. I'm not running

anymore. I'm back."

"For…?"

"For good."

"And your career?"

He exhaled. "I'm not saying I won't miss the travel, but I figure we can do that together. And I'm sure I can get a job with a national…"

"What about the danger? Won't you miss the danger? The excitement? The making a difference?" Afraid to hope, yet unable to prevent herself, Carly waited for his answer.

"I think you provide enough excitement, sweetheart."

Her heart pounded hard inside her chest. "You won't get bored? Miss your old way of life?"

He rubbed his thumb over the pulse point in her wrist. "You are my life. Together we can do things we've never dreamed of alone."

*   *   *

That much was true. It was Mike's strength and belief in her that had gotten her through the last month, even though he wasn't there. She rose and went into the bedroom. When she returned to face Mike, she held out a white box that contained her heart, all wrapped up in one package.

He opened the box and pulled out her manuscript,

handling it as if it was fragile glass. "You did it."

She nodded, watching from a few feet away as he began turning the pages. On page two, she held her breath.

The dedication was burned in her heart and soul. *To the man who told me that passion and love are healthy human emotions. And then set out to prove it.*

Slowly he raised his gaze to meet hers. The golden flecks danced in his eyes. "Thank you," he said softly.

"You're welcome. I couldn't have done it without you. You were right about me... about a lot of things. This is my way of saying thanks." She pointed to the stack of white pages in his hands.

He placed the manuscript back in the box.

"That copy is for you. I hoped... well, if you came back, I wanted you to have it. You can read it if you want," she said, suddenly feeling embarrassed. "There's a lot of me in there."

After meeting with her parents, she'd spent the next two weeks in front of the computer. The heart of the manuscript, the elusive something that had been missing, had miraculously found its way onto the screen. The results had been therapeutic.

"I'll read it because I want to. I already know you."

Afraid to speak because of the lump forming in her throat, and because she was afraid she'd break down, she merely nodded. He had always known her, even when she hadn't known herself.

Taking a deep breath, she gathered her courage and left her past behind. She looked at the man she loved in the eye. "I'm not running anymore either," she whispered.

A harsh groan echoed from deep inside him as he reached for her, pulling her down to the couch with him. He winced but wrapped his arms around her anyway. Lowering his head, his lips met hers. His kiss was wet, hot, everything she remembered and more. Her heart kicked into high gear under the intensity of his kiss.

She lay back on the couch and he followed, bracing his arms on either side of her head. She could see the exertion it took for him to move. "Now tell me," he said, his voice hoarse and disbelieving.

"I love you, Mike. I always have."

"God, I love you, too."

Carly grinned. "Good. Now get up, slowly, and march into that bedroom. I'm taking care of you."

He groaned.

"Someone has to make sure you don't do too much too fast."

He cupped her chin in his hand. "I'm glad that someone is you. Tell me something: When did you realize passion and love were good things?"

"It's silly, really. The night you left and we didn't

make love. It just took me a long time to understand what you'd taught me."

He nibbled on her lower lip. "I'm glad it worked, because it was hell being with you, so close to losing you and walking away without..." He trailed off.

"I understand. When Peter said you were in the hospital and I didn't know what was wrong... I thought I'd lost you without ever having had the chance to tell you that I love you."

"You can't get rid of me that easily. I'm like a bad penny."

She brushed a kiss over his lips. "As long as you keep turning up, my life is complete." Carly paused. "The question is, is yours? I don't want to wake up one day to find that you resent me, that you gave up your career because you thought it was what I wanted... the kind of life Peter would have given me."

He shook his head. "Look at those pictures. You wouldn't have been happy with Peter's kind of staid life. As for me, I lost my parents, remember? Do you really think I'd want my kids to suffer the same fate?"

She blinked and tears rippled down her cheeks. "Kids," she said softly.

"And a dog, and a white picket fence if you want one." He brushed a lone tear aside with his thumb. "I'm through running, sweetheart."

She held her arms open wide. "Unless it's *toward* me.

EPILOGUE

"Life doesn't come with any guarantees. You just put your best foot... I mean paw forward and hope for the best." Mike knelt down and patted the head of the mutt he'd recently rescued from the ASPCA. He'd been covering a story for the local paper about animals that had survived a fire that had taken the lives of their owners.

Surprisingly, he enjoyed the lighter pieces as much as he enjoyed covering harder news. He appreciated the opportunity to do both. But he hadn't expected to get earmarked as a sucker by the first pooch he laid eyes on. He'd been a goner from the minute he'd taken a look at those big brown eyes.

"So there's the paper. Think you can remember that?" Mike asked.

The dog thumped its black tail enthusiastically against the wood floor.

"Good. Now let's hope Carly likes surprises," he said.

He'd left a message for her to meet him here with

good news. Mutt, as he'd come to call him, had accompanied him on his daily run and his easier assignments. So here they were.

Despite the peace and quiet, or perhaps because of it, Mike knew he'd made the right decision. He glanced around at the rambling house that needed as much time and love as this pathetic new pet. He'd have time for both these days. The wandering and danger didn't suit him anymore. The restlessness had begun long before he'd gotten injured on assignment. He just hadn't known the longing was for permanent roots. Who'd have guessed?

Not Carly. She still seemed to be in a daze, as if happiness and security couldn't possibly go hand in hand. As if she was looking for it all to fall apart at any moment.

Mike refilled the mutt's water bowl and placed it on the floor. He understood the source of her fear. Time... and this surprise would prove that they shared something lasting.

The doorbell took him out of his musings and he was grateful for the interruption. The dog didn't react, but then he still hadn't learned to associate the doorbell with human company. Mike headed for the door but didn't miss seeing the dog walk up to the paper and use the floor anyway. He groaned and turned the doorknob, wondering who would ultimately win this battle, him or the pooch.

"Hi."

"Carly."

She smiled, radiating a glow in her cheeks he hadn't seen since... well, never. Talk about progress, he thought.

"Come in," he said.

Carly followed him inside and down a short hall. She'd taken two steps inside the living room when Mike barked out the command. "Stop." She did and looked down, grateful she hadn't gone a step farther. Meeting his gaze, she burst out laughing and stepped around the mess, the paper, but not the dog. How could she, when he insisted on nuzzling her leg with his nose?

She knelt down to give him the attention he craved. "He's cute," she said, tilting her head upward. "And so are you."

He frowned at her description. He'd shaved off the beard weeks ago, but he was still the rebel in attitude and look. He still favored worn jeans that hugged his lean hips and muscled thighs and a black T-shirt that accentuated his biceps.

He was still the man she loved beyond reason. The man she'd marry in a few weeks, in a private, family-only ceremony.

Tearing her gaze from him, she asked, "Okay, what's up? What is this place?" she asked, gesturing around the rambling farmhouse.

He let out a deep breath. "This... is home." He grabbed her hand and led her outside, down a small path to the edge of the property. He patted a peeling post. "And this is your white picket fence."

A smile twitched at the corners of her mouth. "And this is my dog?"

He grinned. "It's the American dream, sweetheart. The house, the dog, the white picket fence..."

"What about the two-point-five kids?" she asked, her eyes dancing with delight.

He leaned forward for a brief but satisfying kiss. "I was hoping one was on its way," he said in a voice he barely recognized.

"If not, I'm sure we can work on it."

Her light, tinkling laughter warmed him. To Mike, it was the sound of promise, of his future. He splayed his hand over her flat stomach. Her hand covered his and the dog nudged at her leg. She laughed again. He wanted to grow old listening to that sound, and he would.

"I like your thinking, and that might take care of one of those kids... but I had something else in mind." She was teasing him and he knew it.

"And here I thought I had all the surprises for today."

She waved papers in front of him. "I did some research, and there's an adoption agency placing orphans from war-ravaged countries. Now I know it's a big responsibility, and I know many of these kids come with problems, but we can handle it. I mean, if you want to."

Did he want to? Give a home to kids who'd lost parents as he had? Only this time, these kids would know love and happiness... and security... Mike glanced back at the old house, and the woman with whom he would make this place a home. He didn't know what he'd done in this life to get so lucky, but he intended to enjoy it.

He took Carly's hand. "I said it from day one: You're something else, sweetheart."

Her eyes glistened with sheer happiness. "So tell me—what's the dog's name?"

Mike paused in thought. "How about Lucky?"

She leaned down to scratch the dog's head. "It sure fits."

Mike grunted and pulled her close. "What do we do with him while we're on our honeymoon?" he murmured in her ear. "He's not paper trained yet remember?"

Carly smiled.

Mike grinned.

"Peter," they both choked out, laughing at the thought.

Carly Phillips

Other Carly Classics

The Right Choice

Suddenly Love (formerly titled Kismet)

Perfect Partners

Unexpected Chances (formerly titled Midnight Angel)

Keep up with Carly and her upcoming books:

Website:
www.carlyphillips.com

Sign up for Carly's Newsletter:
www.carlyphillips.com/newsletter-sign-up

Carly on Facebook:
www.facebook.com/CarlyPhillipsFanPage

Carly on Twitter:
www.twitter.com/carlyphillips

CARLY'S MONTHLY CONTEST!

Visit: www.carlyphillips.com/newsletter-sign-up/ and enter for a chance to win a $25 gift card! You'll also automatically be added to her newsletter list so you can keep up on the newest releases!

If you enjoy books on the steamier side, don't miss my "Dare To Love" series. Read on for an excerpt of Dare to Love…

Dare to Love
Excerpt

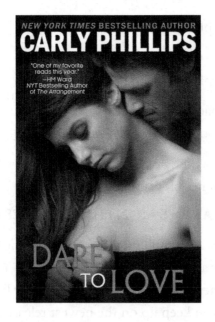

ONE

Once a year, the Dare siblings gathered at the Club Meridian Ballroom in South Florida to celebrate the birthday of the father many of them despised. Ian Dare raised his glass filled with Glenlivet and took a sip, letting the slow burn of fine scotch work its way down his throat and into his system. He'd need another before he fully relaxed.

"Hi, big brother." His sister Olivia strode up to him and nudged him with her elbow.

"Watch the drink," he said, wrapping his free arm around her shoulders for an affectionate hug. "Hi, Olivia."

She returned the gesture with a quick kiss on his cheek. "It's nice of you to be here."

He shrugged. "I'm here for Avery and for you. Although why you two forgave him—"

"Uh-uh. Not here." She wagged a finger in front of his face. "If I have to put on a dress, we're going to act civilized."

Ian stepped back and took in his twenty-four-year-old sister for the first time. Wearing a gold gown, her dark hair up in a chic twist, it was hard to believe she was the same bane of his existence who'd chased after him and his friends until they relented and let her play ball with them.

"You look gorgeous," he said to her.

She grinned. "You have to say that."

"I don't. And I mean it. I'll have to beat men off with sticks when they see you." The thought darkened his mood.

"You do and I'll have your housekeeper short-sheet your bed! Again, there should be perks to getting dressed like this, and getting laid should be one of them."

"I'll pretend I didn't hear that," he muttered and took another sip of his drink.

"You not only promised to come tonight, you swore you'd behave."

Ian scowled. "Good behavior ought to be optional considering the way he flaunts his assets," he said with a nod toward where Robert Dare held court.

Around him sat his second wife of nine years, Savannah Dare, and their daughter, Sienna, along with their nearest and dearest country club friends. Missing were their other two sons, but they'd show up soon.

Olivia placed a hand on his shoulder. "He loves her, you know. And Mom's made her peace."

"Mom had no choice once she found out about *her.*"

Robert Dare had met the much younger Savannah Sheppard and, to hear him tell it, fallen instantly in love. She was now the mother of his three other children, the oldest of whom was twenty-five. Ian had just turned thirty. Anyone could do the math and come up with two families at the same time. The man was beyond fertile, that was for damned sure.

At the reminder, Ian finished his drink and placed the tumbler on a passing server's tray. "I showed my face. I'm out of here." He started for the exit.

"Ian, hold on," his sister said, frustration in her tone.

"What? Do you want me to wait until they sing 'Happy Birthday'? No thanks. I'm leaving."

Before they could continue the discussion, their half brother Alex strode through the double entrance with a spectacular-looking woman holding tightly to his arm, and Ian's plans changed.

Because of *her.*

Some people had presence; others merely wished they possessed that magic something. In her bold, red dress and fuck-me heels, she owned the room. And he wanted to own her. Petite and curvy, with long, chocolate-brown hair that fell down her back in wild curls, she was the antithesis of every too-thin female he'd dated and kept at arm's length. But she was with his half brother, which meant he had to steer clear.

"I thought you were leaving," Olivia said from beside him.

"I am." He should. If he could tear his gaze away from *her*.

"If you wait for Tyler and Scott, you might just relax enough to have fun," she said of their brothers. "Come on, please?" Olivia used the pleading tone he never could resist.

"Yeah, please, Ian? Come on," his sister Avery said, joining them, looking equally mature in a silver gown that showed way too much cleavage. At twenty-two, she was similar in coloring and looks to Olivia, and he wasn't any more ready to think of her as a grown-up—never mind letting other men ogle her—than he was with her sister.

Ian set his jaw, amazed these two hadn't been the death of him yet.

"So what am I begging him to do?" Avery asked Olivia.

Olivia grinned. "I want him to stay and hang out for a while. Having fun is probably out of the question, but I'm trying to persuade him to let loose."

"Brat," he muttered, unable to hold back a smile at Olivia's persistence.

He stole another glance at his lady in red. He could

no more leave than he could approach her, he thought, frustrated because he was a man of action, and right now, he could do nothing but watch her.

"Well?" Olivia asked.

He forced his gaze to his sister and smiled. "Because you two asked so nicely, I'll stay." But his attention remained on the woman now dancing and laughing with his half brother.

*   *   *

Riley Taylor felt his eyes on her from the moment she entered the elegantly decorated ballroom on the arm of another man. As it was, her heels made it difficult enough to maneuver gracefully. Knowing a devastatingly sexy man watched her every move only made not falling on her ass even more of a challenge.

Alex Dare, her best friend, was oblivious. Being the star quarterback of the Tampa Breakers meant he was used to stares and attention. Riley wasn't. And since this was his father's birthday bash, he knew everyone here. She didn't.

She definitely didn't know *him*. She'd managed to avoid this annual party in the past with a legitimate work excuse one year, the flu another, but this year, Alex knew she was down in the dumps due to job problems, and he'd insisted she come along and have a good time.

While Alex danced with his mother then sisters, she headed for the bar and asked the bartender for a glass of ice water. She took a sip and turned to go find a seat, someplace where she could get off her feet and slip free of her offending heels.

She'd barely taken half a step when she bumped into a hard, suit-clad body. The accompanying jolt sent her water spilling from the top of her glass and into her cleavage. The chill startled her as much as the liquid that dripped down her chest.

"Oh!" She teetered on her stilettos, and big, warm hands grasped her shoulders, steadying her.

She gathered herself and looked up into the face of the man she'd been covertly watching. "You," she said on a breathy whisper.

His eyes, a steely gray with a hint of blue in the depths, sparkled in amusement and something more. "Glad you noticed me too."

She blinked, mortified, no words rushing into her brain to save her. She was too busy taking him in. Dark brown hair stylishly cut, cheekbones perfectly carved, and a strong jaw completed the package. And the most intense heat emanated from his touch as he held on to her arms. His big hands made her feel small, not an easy feat when she was always conscious of her too-full curves.

She breathed in deeply and was treated to a masculine, woodsy scent that turned her insides to pure mush. Full-scale awareness rocked her to her core. This man hit all her right buttons.

"Are you all right?" he asked.

"I'm fine." Or she would be if he'd release her so she could think. Instead of telling him so, she continued to stare into his handsome face.

"You certainly are," he murmured.

A heated flush rushed to her cheeks at the compliment, and a delicious warmth invaded her system.

"I'm sorry about the spill," he said.

At least she hoped he was oblivious to her ridiculous attraction to him.

"You're wet." He released her and reached for a napkin from the bar.

Yes, she was. In wholly inappropriate ways considering they'd barely met. Desire pulsed through her veins. Oh my God, what was it about this man that caused reactions in her body another man would have to work overtime to achieve?

He pressed the thin paper napkin against her chest and neck. He didn't linger, didn't stroke her anywhere he shouldn't, but she could swear she felt the heat of his fingertips against her skin. Between his heady scent and his deliberate touch, her nerves felt raw and exposed. Her breasts swelled, her nipples peaked, and she shivered, her body tightening in places she'd long thought dormant. If he noticed, he was too much of a gentleman to say.

No man had ever awakened her senses this way before. Sometimes she wondered if that was a deliberate choice on her part. Obviously not, she thought and forced herself to step back, away from his potent aura.

He crinkled the napkin and placed the paper onto the bar.

"Thank you," she said.

"My pleasure." The word, laced with sexual innuendo, rolled off his tongue, and his eyes darkened, an indication that this crazy attraction she experienced wasn't one-sided.

"Maybe now we can move on to introductions. I'm Ian Dare," he said.

She swallowed hard, disappointment rushing through her as she realized, for all her awareness of him, he was the one man at this party she ought to stay away from. "Alex's brother."

"Half brother," he bit out.

"Yes." She understood his pointed correction. Alex wouldn't want any more of a connection to Ian than Ian did to Alex.

"You have your father's eyes," she couldn't help but note.

His expression changed, going from warm to cold

in an instant. "I hope that's the only thing you think that bastard and I have in common."

Riley raised her eyebrows at the bitter tone. Okay, she understood he had his reasons, but she was a stranger.

Ian shrugged, his broad shoulders rolling beneath his tailored, dark suit. "What can I say? Only a bastard would live two separate lives with two separate families at the same time."

"You do lay it out there," she murmured.

His eyes glittered like silver ice. "It's not like everyone here doesn't know it."

Though she ought to change the subject, he'd been open, so she decided to ask what was on her mind. "If you're still so angry with him, why come for his birthday?"

"Because my sisters asked me to," he said, his tone turning warm and indulgent.

A hint of an easier expression changed his face from hard and unyielding to devastatingly sexy once more.

"Avery and Olivia are much more forgiving than me," he explained.

She smiled at his obvious affection for his siblings. As an only child, she envied them a caring, older brother. At least she'd had Alex, she thought and glanced around looking for the man who'd brought her here. She found him on the dance floor, still with his mother, and relaxed.

"Back to introductions," Ian said. "You know my name; now it's your turn."

"Riley Taylor."

"Alex's girlfriend," he said with disappointment. "I saw you two walk in."

That's what he thought? "No, we're friends. More like brother and sister than anything else."

His eyes lit up, and she caught a glimpse of yet another expression—pleasantly surprised. "That's the best news I've heard all night," he said in a deep, compelling tone, his hot gaze never leaving hers.

At a loss for words, Riley remained silent.

"So, Ms. Riley Taylor, where were you off to in such a hurry?" he asked.

"I wanted to rest my feet," she admitted.

He glanced down at her legs, taking in her red pumps. "Ahh. Well, I have just the place."

Before she could argue—and if she'd realized he'd planned to drag her off alone, she might have—Ian grasped her arm and guided her to the exit at the far side of the room.

"Ian—"

"Shh. You'll thank me later. I promise." He pushed open the door, and they stepped out onto a deck that wasn't in use this evening.

Sticky, night air surrounded them, but being a Floridian, she was used to it, and obviously so was he. His arm still cupping her elbow, he led her to a small love seat and gestured for her to sit.

She sensed he was a man who often got his way, and though she'd never found that trait attractive before, on him, it worked. She settled into the soft cushions. He did the same, leaving no space between them, and she liked the feel of his hard body aligned with hers. Her heart beat hard in her chest, excitement and arousal pounding away inside her.

Around them, it was dark, the only light coming from sconces on the nearby building.

"Put your feet up." He pointed to the table in front of them.

"Bossy," she murmured.

Ian grinned. He was and was damned proud of it. "You're the one who said your feet hurt," he reminded her.

"True." She shot him a sheepish look that was nothing short of adorable.

The reverberation in her throat went straight to Ian's cock, and he shifted in his seat, pure sexual desire now pumping through his veins.

He'd been pissed off and bored at his father's ridiculous birthday gala. Even his sisters had barely been able to coax a smile from him. Then *she'd* walked into the room.

Because she was with his half brother, Ian hadn't planned on approaching her, but the minute he'd caught sight of her alone at the bar, he'd gone after her, compelled by a force beyond his understanding. Finding out she and Alex were just friends had made his night because she'd provide a perfect distraction to the pain that followed him whenever his father's other family was near.

"Shoes?" he reminded her.

She dipped her head and slipped off her heels, moaning in obvious relief.

"That sound makes me think of other things," he said, capturing her gaze.

"Such as?" She unconsciously swayed closer, and he suppressed a grin.

"Sex. With you."

"Oh." Her lips parted with the word, and Ian couldn't tear his gaze away from her lush, red-painted mouth.

A mouth he could envision many uses for, none of them tame.

"Is this how you charm all your women?" she asked. "Because I'm not sure it's working." A teasing smile lifted her lips, contradicting her words.

He had her, all right, as much as she had him.

He kept his gaze on her face, but he wasn't a complete gentleman and couldn't resist brushing his hand over her tight nipples showing through the fabric of her dress.

Her eyes widened in surprise at the same time a soft moan escaped, sealing her fate. He slid one arm across the love seat until his fingers hit her mass of curls, and he wrapped his hand in the thick strands. Then, tugging her close, he sealed his mouth over hers. She opened for him immediately. The first taste was a mere preview, not nearly enough, and he deepened the kiss, taking more.

Sweet, hot, and her tongue tangled with his. He gripped her hair harder, wanting still more. She was like all his favorite vices in one delectable package. Best of all, she kissed him back, every inch a willing, giving partner.

He was a man who dominated and took, but from the minute he tasted her, he gave as well. If his brain were clear, he'd have pulled back immediately, but she reached out and gripped his shoulders, curling her fingers through the fabric of his shirt, her nails digging into his skin. Each thrust of his tongue in her mouth mimicked what he really wanted, and his cock hardened even more.

"You've got to be kidding me," his half brother said, interrupting at the worst possible moment.

He would have taken his time, but Riley jumped,

pushing at his chest and backing away from him at the same time.

"Alex!"

"Yeah. The guy who brought you here, remember?"

Ian cursed his brother's interruption as much as he welcomed the reminder that this woman represented everything Ian resented. His half brother's friend. Alex, with whom he had a rivalry that would have done real siblings proud.

The oldest sibling in the *other* family was everything Ian wasn't. Brash, loud, tattoos on his forearms, and he threw a mean football as quarterback of the Tampa Breakers. Ian, meanwhile, was more of a thinker, president of the Breakers' rivals, the Miami Thunder, owned by his father's estranged brother, Ian's uncle.

Riley jumped up, smoothing her dress and rubbing at her swollen lips, doing nothing to ease the tension emanating from her best friend.

Ian took his time standing.

"I see you met my brother," Alex said, his tone tight.

Riley swallowed hard. "We were just—"

"Getting better acquainted," Ian said in a seductive tone meant to taunt Alex and imply just how much better he now knew Riley.

A muscle ticked in the other man's jaw. "Ready to

go back inside?" Alex asked her.

Neither one of them would make a scene at this mockery of a family event.

"Yes." She didn't meet Ian's gaze as she walked around him and came up alongside Alex.

"Good because my dad's been asking for you. He said it's been too long since he's seen you," Alex said, taunting Ian back with the mention of the one person sure to piss him off.

Despite knowing better, Ian took the bait. "Go on. We were finished anyway," he said, dismissing Riley as surely as she'd done to him.

Never mind that she was obviously torn between her friend and whatever had just happened between them; she'd chosen Alex. A choice Ian had been through before and come out on the same wrong end.

In what appeared to be a deliberately possessive move, Alex wrapped an arm around her waist and led her back inside. Ian watched, ignoring the twisting pain in his gut at the sight. Which was ridiculous. He didn't have any emotional investment in Riley Taylor. He didn't do emotion, period. He viewed relationships through the lens of his father's adultery, finding it easier to remain on the outside looking in.

Distance was his friend. Sex worked for him. It was love and commitment he distrusted. So no matter how different that brief moment with Riley had been, that was all it was.

A moment.

One that would never happen again.

*　　*　　*

Riley followed Alex onto the dance floor in silence. They hadn't spoken a word to each other since she'd let him lead her away from Ian. She understood his shocked reaction and wanted to soothe his frazzled nerves but didn't know how. Not when her own nerves were so raw from one simple kiss.

Except nothing about Ian was simple, and that kiss left her reeling. From the minute his lips touched hers, everything else around her had ceased to matter. The tug of arousal hit her in the pit of her stomach, in her scalp as his fingers tugged her hair, in the weight of her breasts, between her thighs and, most telling, in her mind. He was a strong man, the kind who knew what he wanted and who liked to get his way. The type of man she usually avoided and for good reason.

But she'd never experienced chemistry so strong before. His pull was so compelling she'd willingly followed him outside regardless of the fact that she knew without a doubt her closest friend in the world would be hurt if she got close to Ian.

"Are you going to talk to me?" Alex asked, breaking into her thoughts.

"I'm not sure what to say."

On the one hand, he didn't have a say in her personal life. She didn't owe him an apology. On the other, he was her everything. The child she'd grown up next door to and the best friend who'd saved her sanity and given her a safe haven from her abusive father.

She was wrong. She knew exactly what to say. "I'm sorry."

He touched his forehead to hers. "I don't know what came over me. I found you two kissing, and I saw red."

"It was just chemistry." She let out a shaky laugh, knowing that term was too benign for what had passed between her and Ian.

"I don't want you to get hurt. The man doesn't do relationships, Ri. He uses women and moves on."

"Umm, Pot/Kettle?" she asked him. Alex moved from woman to woman just as he'd accused his half brother of doing.

He'd even kissed *her* once. Horn dog that he was, he said he'd had to try, but they both agreed there was no spark and their friendship meant way too much to throw away for a quick tumble between the sheets.

Alex frowned. "Maybe so, but that doesn't change the facts about him. I don't want you to get hurt."

"I won't," she assured him, even as her heart

picked up speed when she caught sight of Ian watching them from across the room.

Drink in hand, brooding expression on his face, his stare never wavered.

She curled her hands into the suit fabric covering Alex's shoulders and assured herself she was telling the truth.

"What if he was using you to get to me?"

"Because the man can't be interested in me for me?" she asked, her pride wounded despite the fact that Alex was just trying to protect her.

Alex slowed his steps and leaned back to look into her eyes. "That's not what I meant, and you know it. Any man would be lucky to have you, and I'd never get between you and the right guy." A muscle pulsed in Alex's right temple, a sure sign of tension and stress. "But Ian's not that guy."

She swallowed hard, hating that he just might be right. Riley wasn't into one-night stands. Which was why her body's combustible reaction to Ian Dare confused and confounded her. How far would she have let him go if Alex hadn't interrupted? Much further than she'd like to imagine, and her body responded with a full-out shiver at the thought.

"Now can we forget about him?"

Not likely, she thought, when his gaze burned hotter than his kiss. Somehow she managed to swallow over the lump in her throat and give Alex the answer he sought. "Sure."

Pleased, Alex pulled her back into his arms to continue their slow dance. Around them, other guests, mostly his father's age, moved slowly in time to the music.

"Did I mention how much I appreciate you coming here with me?" Obviously trying to ease the tension between them, he shot her the same charming grin that had women thinking they were special.

Riley knew better. She *was* special to him, and if he ever turned his brand of protectiveness on the right kind of woman and not the groupies he preferred, he might find himself settled and happy one day. Sadly, he didn't seem to be on that path.

She decided to let their disagreement over Ian go. "I believe you've mentioned how wonderful I am a couple of times. But you still owe me one," Riley said. Parties like this weren't her thing.

"It took your mind off your job stress, right?" he asked.

She nodded. "Yes, and let's not even talk about that right now." Monday was soon enough to deal with her new boss.

"You got it. Ready for a break?" he asked.

She nodded. Unable to help herself, she glanced over where she'd seen Ian earlier, but he was gone.

The disappointment twisting the pit of her stomach was disproportional to the amount of time she'd known him, and she blamed that kiss.

Her lips still tingled, and if she closed her eyes and ran her tongue over them, she could taste his heady, masculine flavor. Somehow she had to shake him from her thoughts. Alex's reaction to seeing them together meant Riley couldn't allow herself the luxury of indulging in anything more with Ian.

Not even in her thoughts or dreams.

About the Author

N.Y. Times and *USA Today* Bestselling Author Carly Phillips has written over 40 sexy contemporary romance novels. After a successful 15 year career with various New York publishing houses, Carly made the leap to Indie author, with the goal of giving her readers more books at a faster pace at a better price. Carly lives in Purchase, NY with her family, two nearly adult daughters and two crazy dogs who star on her Facebook Fan Page and website. She's a writer, a knitter of sorts, a wife, and a mom. In addition, she's a Twitter and Internet junkie and is always around to interact with her readers.

CARLY'S BOOKLIST
by Series

Below are links to my series on my website
where you will find buy links for each novel!

Dare to Love Series
(www.carlyphillips.com/category/books/?series=dare-to-love)

Dare to Love

Dare to Desire

Dare to Surrender

Dare to Submit

Dare to Touch (coming January 2015)

Look for more Dare to Love series books in 2015!

Other Carly Classics

The Right Choice

Suddenly Love (formerly titled Kismet)

Perfect Partners

Unexpected Chances (formerly titled Midnight Angel)

Carly's Earlier Traditionally Published Books

Serendipity Series
(www.carlyphillips.com/category/books/?series=serendipity-series)

Serendipity

Destiny

Karma

Serendipity's Finest Series
(www.carlyphillips.com/category/books/?series=serendipitys-finest)

Perfect Fit

Perfect Fling

Perfect Together

Serendipity Novellas
(www.carlyphillips.com/category/books/?series=serendipity-novellas)

Fated

Hot Summer Nights (Perfect Stranger)

Bachelor Blog Series
(www.carlyphillips.com/category/books/?series=bachelor-blog-series)

Kiss Me If You Can

Love Me If You Dare

Lucky Series
(www.carlyphillips.com/category/books/?series=lucky-series)

Lucky Charm

Lucky Streak

Lucky Break

Ty and Hunter Series
(www.carlyphillips.com/category/books/?series=ty-hunter-series)

Cross My Heart

Sealed with a Kiss

Hot Zone Series
(www.carlyphillips.com/category/books/?series=hot-zone-series)

Hot Stuff

Hot Number

Hot Item

Hot Property

Costas Sisters Series
(www.carlyphillips.com/category/books/?series=costas-sisters-series)

Summer Lovin'

Under the Boardwalk

Chandler Brothers Series
(www.carlyphillips.com/category/books/?series=chandler-brothers-series)

The Bachelor

The Playboy

The Heartbreaker

Stand Alone Titles
(www.carlyphillips.com/category/books/?series=other-books)

Brazen

Seduce Me

Secret Fantasy